HEART THIEF, BLUEGRASS SECURITY BOOK ONE

PJ FIALA

ROLLING THUNDER PUBLISHING

Printed in the United States of America

First published 2016 - Republished 2019

Fiala, PJ

HEART THIEF / PJ Fiala

p. cm.

ISBN: 978-1-942618-44-7

1. Romance—Fiction. 2. Romance—Suspense. 3. Romance - Military

GET A FREE EBOOK!

Building a relationship with my readers is the very best thing about writing. I send monthly newsletters with details on new releases, special offers and other fun things relating to my books or prizes surrounding them.

If you sign up to my mailing list I'll send you:

1. A copy of Moving to Love, Book 1 of the Rolling Thunder series.

2. A book list so you know what order to read my books in.

You can get Moving to Love **for free**, by signing up at https://www.subscribepage.com/PJsReadersClub_copy

ALSO BY PJ FIALA

Click here to see a list of all of my books with the blurbs.

Rory: Finding His Match Book Four

GHOST

Defending Keirnan, GHOST Prequel

Defending Sophie, GHOST Book One

Defending Roxanne, GHOST Book Two

Defending Yvette, GHOST Book Three

DEDICATION

I've had so many wonderful people come into my life, and I want you all to know how much I appreciate you. From each and every reader who takes the time out of their day to read my stories and leave reviews, thank you.
My beta readers, Anita, Barbara, and Teresa; ladies, thank you so very much for your suggestions, praise, and time.
Thank you to my proofreader, Sara - I appreciate you.

Graphics by Stacy designed this gorgeous cover and I couldn't be happier - thank you Stacy.

And a special thank you to my business manager Chas and her team for keeping things rolling along, making suggestions to enhance my business and being a sounding board.

Last, but not least, my family for the love and sacrifices they've made and continue to make to help me achieve this dream—especially my husband and best friend,

Gene. Words can never express how much you mean
to me.

To our veterans and currently serving members of our
armed forces and police departments; thank you, ladies
and gentlemen, for your hard work and sacrifices. It's with
gratitude and thankfulness that I mention you in this
forward.

1

The weather had turned colder today; typical Nebraska weather—cool one day, warm the next. Pulling his stiff hands from his woolen coat pockets, Levi opened the door to the diner, and the warmth washed over him comingled with the delicious aromas of freshly baked biscuits and bacon frying in the kitchen. Nodding to the waitress, he found a seat in the booth in the corner—his favorite place. It was hard staying to yourself in this town. Everybody knew everyone and everything a person did; it was annoying. Although, in his line of work, it did come in handy to know some of the things going on. He tried to quietly keep tabs on everything within reason.

The waitress walked to his table, a skip in her step and a cheery smile. It was a bit too early in the day for that as far as he was concerned. She smiled brightly. "Mornin', Levi. The usual today?"

"Morning, Viv. Black coffee, two eggs over easy, an order of crispy bacon, and toast on the side."

She jotted something on her order form, then offered, "Yep, the usual. Be right back with your coffee."

She skipped away, and he took the opportunity to glance at her legs. She always wore shorts and tennis shoes when she worked. Her nail polish was always a different color and her red hair was always pulled up in some messy-looking do. She dressed a bit too young for her age—which he guessed to be mid-forties, maybe fifties—and she still maintained the vigor of youth. Whereas, he felt old beyond his forty-five years.

He frowned as he watched her briskly move behind the counter; she was a whirlwind of activity—smiling and waving—just a happy gal. He slightly shook his head as he glanced around the diner. The usual suspects were present this morning. Some of the older farmers gathered each morning to talk about crops, equipment, and to gossip about the goings-on in town. There was an elderly couple at the next booth, a couple of high school kids at one of the tables, a nice looking younger gal with long dark hair and a striking face at the table in the window, and a smattering of truck drivers at the counter. This week's gossip was especially juicy because the Halloween Festival was coming up next week and that's when the majority of the town's shenanigans happened. As soon as you added a haunted house, zombie shooting, a kissing booth, and a tarot reader to a small town, things that normally didn't occur began to happen.

It was sure as hell going to make his job harder this week. He hoped his new guy, Sage Reynolds, who should be arriving this afternoon—worked out. He'd started his security firm a couple of years ago, and he was finally starting to see some profit. Worried that profit would float away if this new guy and Chuck, his employee of about two weeks, didn't get trained to take on some of his work, Levi heaved out a heavy sigh.

"Here's your usual, Levi." Viv set the steaming plate of bacon and eggs in front of him, his toast on the side on a separate plate, two pats of butter next to the toast, a little pot of apricot jam next to that, and she refilled his coffee cup. She seemed to have five arms, though by looking at her, you'd never guess she could carry a kitchen full of food in one trip through the diner.

"Thanks, Viv."

"You're welcome. Are you excited for the festival? It's my favorite time of year. Ooh, and did you hear? We're going to have a gypsy in town. I hope she can read my palm and tell me something good."

In spite of trying to stay neutral, he chuckled. "What would be something good?"

"Oh, you know. Love, marriage, house with a picket fence, a dog—the works."

"I find it hard to believe you don't already have all those things."

She smiled brightly and winked. "Not yet, and at my age, time's a wastin', but I'm still hopeful."

He glanced briefly at her backside as she moved to the next table to refill their coffee cups. She sauntered back before he'd finished his eggs and checked on the quality of the food, quietly laid the newspaper alongside his plates, and walked away without another word.

He opened the paper to glance at the local goings-on and frowned when he saw there'd been another break-in at one of the farms. The locals had a hard time letting go of the old ways of doing things and private security seemed a bit uppity and unnecessary to some of them. They thought they knew about everything going on in this town and private security or security cameras weren't something that was needed. Luckily enough, there had been new people moving into town as of late, and they were from areas where security cameras, microphones, and devices were necessary. That's how he flourished. That and locals in the next town over—in York—loved his work.

He trained his ears on the old farmers jabbering next to him and heard them speaking of the break-in. Oddly, they had more information than what was printed in the paper. Food, clothing, tools, and some pry bars had been taken from Thomas Bennett's barn.

Finishing his coffee, he watched the gal sitting in front of the window. She sat quietly enough, but she was assessing the crowd. He watched as she looked at each table and booth occupant before moving on to the next. When her eyes landed on his, a little jolt ran through his body; those dark eyes of hers were mesmerizing. She was petite of build, but intelligence showed on her face and in the way she held herself. She wore no makeup on her face and yet she was striking. Their gazes locked for a few moments, then she glanced to the farmers sitting at the big table next to his.

He tucked the paper under his arm and walked to the cash register at the end of the counter, laid the paper down, and pulled his wallet from his back pocket.

"Busy day ahead, Levi?"

"Yeah. I just hired a new guy to help me out and maybe train Chuck. Hoping it all works as planned."

"Okay, good luck then. If you need a date for the festival, I might be available." She smiled her brightest smile, and he couldn't help but grin back. "Thanks, Viv, but I'll be working the festival this year. TJ asked me to head up security around town." TJ Bennett was the Mayor of Sapphire Falls and the oldest of the boys in the Bennett family. Levi had been surprised but thrilled when TJ called him about security.

"Well, look at you working with the Mayor and all." She let out a low whistle and Levi blushed.

$\sim$

Sage Reynolds sat at the table in the window at the diner in Sapphire Falls. The last thing she'd wanted to do was end up in another small town like the one she'd just left. There'd be no prospects for jobs, dating, fun or anything, and the fact that small towns were nothing more than gossip holes and a place where fun went to die. Fifteen years in the Army meant she was ready for life on her terms.

She was fortunate, though, that she'd found this job. Her last email was a late notice from her credit card company, and she needed the money. Burying her father eight months ago, wrapping up his paltry estate and selling off his old furniture, record collection, and the fifty-seven Buick he'd restored was behind her now. She'd burned through her savings on her dad's medical bills and medications before he died, so she had some catching up to do.

When the offer from LJS came in for a security position, she had no choice but to take it. They'd agreed to start out on a two-week trial and see if they could work together to get LJS through the Halloween Festival. She'd agreed simply because of the two-week trial. She'd continue to send out her resume in the meantime and get out of this small town for good and land in a big city, maybe Minneapolis. San Diego would be fantastic, and warm. She liked it warm.

Glancing around the diner, she noticed each of the customers sitting and shooting the breeze, all of them gossiping about someone named Mary Borcher and her penchant for booze. The haunted house seemed to be a place where folks went to make out. A ride on the Ferris wheel seemed to mean you were going steady, and if you got a kiss on it, it was serious. Small towns!

She glanced at the handsome man in the back of the diner, sandy brown graying hair—ex-military, for sure—rigid posture and constantly assessing the crowd. Loner. No wedding ring, quiet, and he liked to glance over the paper as he listened to the conversations going on around him.

"Can I get you something else, sugar?" The waitress was chipper and bubbly.

Clearing her throat, Sage said, "No thanks. But can you tell me if you have a bed and breakfast or a hotel in town?"

Viv set the coffeepot on the table and pulled her order pad from her apron. She wrote something quickly on it and ripped the page off, handing it to Sage.

"This is the bed and breakfast in town; it's called the Rise & Shine. Austin Stone is the new owner and the place is clean and friendly. You should have no problem getting a room this time of year. Tell them Viv sent you from Dottie's. It's just the next street over." She pointed with her thumb over her shoulder.

Sage glanced at the neat penmanship and the name, address, and phone number of the B&B. "Thank you so much. It means a lot to me."

"Sure thing, darlin'. How long are you staying?"

Folding the paper and sliding it in her jacket pocket, she replied, "Two weeks."

"Oh, well, you'll be here for the festival then. I hope you'll check it out; it's so much fun, and if you don't mind me saying, the single men would certainly line up for a kiss with you at the kissing booth."

Sage blushed to the roots of her hair. "Um, I don't think I'll have time for kissing booths or kissing men, but thank you."

"Never rule it out, darlin'." Viv winked, and Sage held out her hand.

"Sorry for my manners; my name is Sage Reynolds."

Shaking hands, Viv smiled sweetly. "Nice to meet you, Sage Reynolds. Stop in while you're here and if you need a tour guide, let me know; I'm happy to assist. I get off work just after the lunch hour and have my afternoons free."

"Thank you." Sage pulled a twenty from her jacket pocket and laid it on the table. "Do I pay you or at the register?"

"Either is fine, sugar. I'll be right back." Picking up the coffeepot and scrambling to the register, Viv stopped to refill cups along the way.

Sage stood and pulled her duffel bag from under the table, pulled on her gloves, and hoisted her bag onto her shoulder. Viv came back and handed her change and Sage promptly pulled out the twenty percent for a tip and dropped the rest in her pocket. She made her way to the door, careful not to bean anyone in the head with her big duffel. Stepping onto the sidewalk, she inhaled the crisp air deeply into her lungs and let it out slowly. Everyone had been nice so far, but it felt stifling to her. It was going to be a long two weeks.

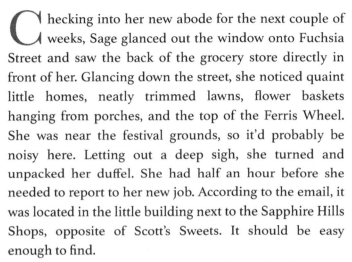

C hecking into her new abode for the next couple of weeks, Sage glanced out the window onto Fuchsia Street and saw the back of the grocery store directly in front of her. Glancing down the street, she noticed quaint little homes, neatly trimmed lawns, flower baskets hanging from porches, and the top of the Ferris Wheel. She was near the festival grounds, so it'd probably be noisy here. Letting out a deep sigh, she turned and unpacked her duffel. She had half an hour before she needed to report to her new job. According to the email, it was located in the little building next to the Sapphire Hills Shops, opposite of Scott's Sweets. It should be easy enough to find.

Tucking her duffel bag into the closet, she glanced at herself in the mirror, shrugged her shoulders, deciding she looked good enough for reporting to work, and made her way downstairs to begin her walk to LJS.

2

S tanding in front of the door to LJS, Sage took a deep breath. She needed this job; she had to keep reminding herself of this fact. Once it was over, she could head south and open her own security firm and walk her own path. Opening and closing her fists, she dipped her head and continued.

She opened the door and stepped into the office. The atmosphere was...non-existent. Pale green walls, two metal desks from the fifties strewn with papers and empty coffee cups sat to the left of the front door. To the right was a little rolling cart with a coffee maker, sugar and creamer, both of which had been spilled and not wiped up, and a stack of Styrofoam cups. The wooden coat rack screwed to the wall next to the door was graced with one coat and three empty brass hooks. Her stomach dropped. Living in various Army barracks over the years, the one thing drilled into her head was neat and tidy. Orderly. Unplanned inspections kept her on her toes.

A creak sounded, and she turned to see the man from the diner sitting behind one of the desks, his soft brown eyes sizing her up. She watched as his eyes traveled the length of her body, not in an overtly sexual way, just an assessment. Probably trying to determine if she was armed. She smirked when she saw the recognition register on his face. She stepped forward and held out her hand.

"Sage Reynolds reporting for duty. I assume you're Levi Jacobson."

His brows raised into his hairline, his jaw tensed, and his back turned rigid. "Is this some sort of joke?" His voice was deep, edgy, and tinged with unhappiness.

"Excuse me? Joke?" She tried keeping the edge from her voice but apparently wasn't all that successful by the look on his face.

He stood, and instead of taking her hand, he placed his firmly on his hips. "I hired a man named Sage Reynolds to work security here with me."

The snark tinted her voice. "You hired me—Sage Reynolds. We never discussed my gender. Quite frankly, it shouldn't matter. I'm trained, dependable, reliable, and ready to work with you. For two weeks, that is."

He took a deep breath, seemingly to keep his irritation in check. "I don't think this is a job for a woman. I hired a security specialist. A black belt in Jujitsu. An expert in surveillance."

She placed her hands on her hips and dug her fingers in to keep herself in check. She needed a job and a paycheck. "Maybe not *any* woman. But then again, I'm not like most women. I'm your security, Jujitsu black belt, and surveillance specialist." Her heart hammered. Sexist. Figured.

The door opened, and a cool blast of air circled the room and turned up the corners of the papers sitting on

Levi's desk. A large man breezed into the room. That is, he breezed as much as a man his size could breeze. He was six-foot-four, broad as a refrigerator, and weighed about 320 pounds. He had sparkling blue eyes and blond hair in need of a trim, but he had a face that looked...happy.

He skirted around Sage and stopped at the coffee maker. Pouring a cup, he laced it with sugar and turned toward her. He glanced down to her Army boots and then back up to her eyes. A big smile creased his face as he held out his hand. "Chuck."

She turned to face him head on, glanced at his offered hand and placed hers in it. She squeezed as she shook his hand. A firm handshake is the best introduction you can give someone her father would say. "Sage."

Chuck's eyes grew big and round. With disbelief in his voice, he said, "You're the new guy?" He turned his gaze to the man behind the desk.

"She's not working here," he clipped out.

"You hired me to do a job, yet you're firing me because I'm a woman? I'd say you're a sexist and about ready to be served with a lawsuit."

Chuck pleaded, "Levi, let's just see what she can do. I need help at the Timmons house; I'm too big to squeeze into some of the places where the wires need to go."

"No." Levi glanced out the window, his jaw ticking as he ground his teeth together.

His phone rang, and he grabbed it from his pocket without looking at either of them. "LJS."

Sage watched with narrowed eyes as Levi spoke into the phone, which clearly didn't sound like a great call.

"Okay, I'll get someone out there today." He practically punched his phone to turn it off, then dropped it soundly on his desk. Taking another cleansing breath, he glanced at Chuck. "Did you finish the job at the Vanderlaydens'?"

Chuck's cheeks tinted pink. Quietly, he admitted, "No."

"So, Timmons' isn't finished, Vanderlaydens' isn't finished, and we have some planning to do for the festival. I have to be out at three separate houses in York. And, I just got an email from two new potential customers who are worried about the break-ins and want cameras installed in their barns."

He stepped from behind the desk, stalked over to the coffee maker, poured a cup, and drank quickly. Sage watched him process this predicament and noticed that he had one shoe with a very thick sole on it, the other without. She landed her gaze on his eyes and saw that he was watching her. He rubbed the back of his neck with his free hand then rotated his head. She heard him mutter, "Shit."

3

Just what he needed—a woman. He needed to have to babysit a woman like he needed a third tit. By the looks of her, she couldn't fight her way out of a paper bag, but she wanted him to believe she had a black belt and was a security specialist? Seriously.

He was having a hard enough time finding the hours needed to train Chuck which, apparently, was going to have to be now. He'd hired the big man because of his size and enthusiasm. He seemed to have a good head on his shoulders and was willing to learn. But when it came to things that took finesse and a smaller build, he wasn't the man for the job.

"Boss, I could really use her. If she can help me with the finer things needed, I can get the two outstanding jobs finished and begin with the new ones. Honest."

Levi watched Chuck look at Sage, hope in his eyes. Her jaw was set tight, her posture tall and proud, and her lips clenched together. He glanced out the window once more, looking at nothing in particular, but seeing people walking by on the sidewalk chattering away.

Her voice had an edge to it, but it sounded to him like the sultry notes a lounge singer would lovingly emit on stage. "Look, apparently, for some strange reason, you thought I was a man. Not sure where that idea came from. You liked my qualifications well enough to hire me sight unseen. I haven't lied about anything. I've spent the past fifteen years in the Army serving as a human intelligence collector. The past year was spent taking care of and then burying my father. I need a job; you need help. It's just for two weeks."

Levi leveled his gaze on her. She was petite of build—Chuck's polar opposite—dark brown eyes similar to the black coffee he was drinking, and the confidence of Vladimir Putin. It was crazy to hire her on. But, dammit, he needed the help.

Letting out another deep breath, he simply nodded. To Chuck, he said, "Get the jobs done and nothing more. Teach her what she needs, and then get back here so we can go over the plans of the park and where we're going to need to set up for the festival."

Chuck's smile spread wide and shown bright as he looked at Levi. "Thanks, Boss." He set his coffee cup on the second littered desk and waved his hand toward Sage. "Let's go before he changes his mind."

As Chuck and Sage closed the office door, Levi limped to his desk, his leg giving him fits of pain as the colder weather set in. He opened the right drawer on his desk and pulled out the anti-inflammatory he took, popped the top and tossed a pill into his mouth, washing it down with the coffee in his cup. He glanced into the last drink of his coffee and thought again of the color of Sage's eyes. The jacket she wore swallowed her up, making her appear smaller rather than larger. He suspected she tried looking bigger than she was by wearing it. What kind of woman wore Army boots outside of the Army, anyway?

He slugged the last bit of coffee and tossed the empty cup in the wastebasket alongside his desk and grabbed his phone and the files on the homes he'd be visiting today. Grabbing his jacket from the hook on the wall, he flipped the switch on the lights, stepped out into the crisp fall air, and locked the door.

4

"What's his problem?" Sage tried to keep her tone light, but she was pissed. She fastened her seat belt and glanced at the office window, seeing Levi plop down into his desk chair. So much for a welcome to LJS, Sapphire Falls, or anything. She'd just driven from Indianapolis to Nebraska, and he barely acknowledged her sacrifice—just because she wasn't a man. *Jerk.*

Chuck started his truck, then turned to smile at her. "Don't worry about him; he doesn't like women much. But if you can show him you know what you're talking about, you can turn him around."

Crossing her arms in front of her, she snapped out, "I don't need to turn him around."

Chuck ceased in putting the truck in drive and looked at her. He turned his whole body toward her, from the waist up and looked into her eyes. His were blue like a summer sky and framed with thick brown lashes. Girls probably envied those lashes; she did. "Yeah, you do. You see, here's how I see this working. He received a Dear John letter while he was deployed to Iraq which was, what, like thirteen or fourteen years ago now. It hit him hard because she married his former best friend. He grabbed hold of that betrayal and won't let go."

Tamping down the sorry she was feeling for him, she let her hurt feelings continue to rest on the surface of her mood. "Don't see how that has a thing to do with me, ya know?"

Chuck tilted his head to the side, "Where's that from? Ya know?"

She shrugged. "Here and there."

He chuckled and his face transformed into a beautiful sight. He was handsome in his own way, boyish and charming—disarming for a big guy. Not her type, which was a good thing because it seemed he was going to be her new best friend while she was here. "It has a lot to do with you. For whatever reason, God has sent you here. I haven't had a ton of time to figure it out or think more about it, but the way I see it, He's using you as a tool." He pointed to the top of the truck meaning Heaven. "It's about time Levi learned that not all women are untrustworthy. I saw how you stood up to him in there."

He turned and put the truck in gear, looked over his left shoulder and eased them out into traffic. "You're the one to do it."

Sage turned her head to the right and watched the little town pass by her window as she processed his comments. She didn't have the time or energy right now to make a pigheaded chauvinist change his mind about women. Period. Two weeks and she was gone—once she got her paycheck, that is.

"So, let me tell you what we have going on today, and thank you for coming along to help me. I didn't know what I was going to do and I want this job. I don't want to go back to farming; it isn't for me."

She listened to Chuck chatter on about the two jobs they had to complete today. Seemed that she'd be climbing behind, under and around tiny spaces to finish feeding and connecting wires for the newly installed security systems he'd started. She had so much more knowledge to offer than just being the little person to climb around things. *Two weeks.* It seemed that would be her new mantra.

5

"Jacobson!" Levi barked into his phone. He'd rapped his knuckles more than a few times today, and they were sore and bleeding. He had a headache and his leg hurt like a bitch. He was in a sour mood and his gut churned at what all this meant for his business. A woman. Shit.

"Whoa. Bad day?" The voice of his best friend, Sam McKenzie, laughingly teased.

Levi stood from his bent position, securing a wire around a window molding and pinched the bridge of his nose. "Yeah. What's up with you?"

"I thought I'd come to visit this week; that is, if you have time for me."

Levi's head swam. He stifled the groan that threatened because he hadn't seen McKenzie in months. But, he was up to his ass in work and not enough help to see it through. "Mac, there's nothing I'd like more, but I may have to put you to work."

The hearty laugh at the other end of the line was like

listening to your favorite piece of music. "You can put me to work; I wanted to talk to you about work anyway."

He let his eyes travel to the window he'd just hidden the wires around and mentally noted one area where they were still visible. Glancing out the window, he winced when his work truck and his two newest employees pulled up the long gravel driveway. "What about work?"

"Nope, not now. Talk to you tomorrow morning. I trust I can bed down at your place? No ladies wandering about, are there?"

Letting out a long breath, he bit his tongue so the retort he wanted to let loose didn't actually come out of his mouth. Old Mrs. James would be scarred for life if she heard him.

"Mac. Don't."

Laughter from the other end of the phone suddenly seemed less like music and more like fingernails on a chalkboard. "Okay. See you in the morning. I'm flying in around seven-thirty. I've got a rental car ready, and I'll be there around eight."

"Seems you planned all of this before calling."

He ended the call to the raucous laughing at the other end and stepped outside to see what Chuck and Sage were doing here. As he reached the truck, they stepped out laughing. Chuck's cheeks were bright pink, and Sage's face was...stunning. It irritated him that her clothes were dusty, her jeans had smudges and streaks on them from crawling around floors and in attics, but her dark hair was pulled back into a low ponytail allowing him to clearly see her features—tiny nose, clear skin, and deep brown eyes. But what struck him most was the smile on her face transformed the tense mug he'd seen earlier to a vision he couldn't look away from. She was simply extraordinary, even in men's clothing.

"Boss, we finished in record time because of Sage and thought we'd come out and help you. She's fast, she's efficient, and she already knows our G-eighteen system."

Levi glanced her way and the smile immediately left her face. He was sorry that he'd caused her to mar her gorgeous face for a second.

"How do you know about the G-eighteen?"

She put her hands on her slender hips and squared herself up to him. "It isn't like you're the only security company that uses the G-eighteen. I've studied up on it extensively. When I own my own company, it's the system I intend to use."

Levi raised his brows. "You're going to own your own company someday?"

"Yes."

He smirked, but Chuck chimed in before he could respond. "That is so cool. You'll do good in your own company, Sage. Honest." He scraped his hands through his unruly hair, the big smile on his face eclipsing the fraction of tension that had just reared up.

Sage glanced at Chuck, and the blinding smile she graced him with made Levi envious. "Thanks, Chuck. If you get tired of small town life, you can come with me."

His eyes rounded. "Really? Awesome."

The easy friendship they'd struck up while working together made Levi a tad jealous. He guarded himself, and it took someone a long time to break down his defenses.

"Okay, I've got to finish this job up." He turned to Sage, "Since you're a G-eighteen expert, why don't you finish installing the software while Chuck and I finish the wiring."

He turned without waiting for an answer and strode to the house.

6

Trudging up the steps at the Rise & Shine, Sage pulled the hair band from her hair. Tangling her fingers in the snarls, she grimaced as she wearily unlocked the door and entered her room.

The fresh smell of clean spring fresh sheets and orange furniture polish instantly relaxed her. It reminded her of her parents' home as she was growing up. She shrugged out of her jacket and sat on the edge of the old wooden bed to remove her boots. She flopped back, and the old wood creaked, causing her to smile. Her grandma's old bed squeaked when she'd crawl up on it. Staring up at the ceiling, she noticed for the first time the intricate scroll painting around the edges of the white ceiling and the antique light fixture of brass and crystals hanging in the middle.

Levi was a puzzle right now and darn it if she didn't like figuring out puzzles. He was a sexy silver fox too, with the smattering of gray at his temples and dusted throughout his sandy brown hair. His soft brown eyes reminded her of toffee. Sad toffee, if there was such a thing. If he'd just smile, his face would be swoon worthy. Too bad he was an ass.

She sat upright and began pulling her clothing off to shower. Her emotions had been all over the place today—nervous, excited, pissed off, and then she'd had fun with Chuck. He was nice, handsome, and funny. They'd told jokes and stories and chatted most of the day. He was like the big brother she'd never had, or one of the guys she'd spent so much time with in the Army.

Turning the shower on to warm the water, she pulled her favorite gray sweats and a pink long-sleeve t-shirt from her duffle, leaving it on the bed to unpack. She grabbed a pair of panties and a bra, then stepped into the bathroom to wash the day away and start over.

Drying her hair, she heard her cell phone ring from the bedroom. She quickly grabbed it from the bed and answered on the third ring.

"Reynolds."

"Hey, Sage, it's Chuck. Levi's buying us dinner so we can eat while we go over the plat maps and plans for the festival. What do you like to eat?"

"A burger and fries sounds good."

"Levi has a friend coming into town tomorrow. I'm kinda stoked. I'll get all kinds of training from two people."

She giggled, "See you in a bit, Chuck."

She tossed her phone on the bed and finished drying her hair, opting for a high ponytail. She replaced her sweats with clean jeans and tucked the pink t-shirt into her jeans and tugged at the shirt by her waist to blouson it out and hide her tiny breasts—her worst feature. She grabbed her hoodie from the closet, skipped down the steps. Not meeting anyone on the way, she wondered just how many guests were here right now. The place sure was quiet. She walked across the grass behind the grocery store and out to the street, studying the bank as she walked by. It was a sturdy looking building made of brick and somehow it looked friendly. Next to the bank was the post office—neat and tidy. The whole town was tidy, and the trees all wore beautiful crimson hues. At the base of the trees were colorful blankets of leaves accenting the green of the grass and creating a kaleidoscope of color throughout the town. The fresh, crisp air was clean, and was that pumpkin pie she smelled? Must be from the diner.

Her stomach rumbled, bringing her attention to the fact that she hadn't eaten in a few hours. To make it worse, she walked past Scott's Sweets, and darn it, that smelled like chocolaty goodness and her mouth watered. Tomorrow she was stopping in there to get her and Chuck something yummy to snack on in the truck.

She opened the door to LJS and found Levi sitting at his desk, a grimace on his face as he looked at his computer screen. Even with his mouth turned down, he was handsome. Wasn't fair. She looked at the hand covering the mouse. She loved manly hands, and his were manly. Strong thick fingers, and a dusting of fine hairs on the backs. She took in his face and saw fine lines around his eyes, faint creases in his forehead, and it all made for a face with character and one which held many hurts and fears.

Her eyes darted to the screen, and it looked blank. Unable to control herself, she said, "You have to turn it on to make it work."

He darted his eyes her way, then glanced at his

computer again before sarcastically replying, "Really?
That must be what's wrong. You're a genius."

She hung her hoodie on one of the hooks behind the
door and walked toward the desk, a grin on her face.
"Nothing genius about it, Boss. Where's Chuck?"

"Getting food."

He wiggled the mouse and turned the monitor off and
back on. "Dammit," He muttered.

She debated standing and watching him work
through this, but she was a bit unnerved by him. His aftershave floated to her, and butterflies set flight in her
tummy. Dammit! Smells left imprints on her brain, and
he smelled fabulous. Something clean and spicy. Her
hands shook a bit, and she tucked her fingers into the
front pockets of her jeans. "Do you need help with
something?"

"Damn thing just shut off in the middle of doing a
bid."

She tentatively stepped forward, not sure how far she
should push. "May I?"

He looked at her—really looked at her—for the first
time since she'd walked in the door. His eyes instantly
found hers and held for a few moments. Her heartbeat
increased, and she swallowed the lump in her throat. She
waited for a sarcastic retort, but he surprised her, his eyes
still holding hers. "Do you know about computers?"

"A bit. I've dealt with a few issues here and there and
can work through most things. I used to date a guy who
was a super geek."

When he continued to stare at her, she thought his
eyes took on a different color, deeper brown and rich in
hue. Finally, he stood and pushed his chair away from the
desk. He stepped away and she noticed him limp. He

walked toward her and held his hand out toward his desk, "If you think you can do something with it, please do."

He walked toward a counter in the back of the room, under which was a small refrigerator. What she shouldn't have noticed was his fine backside, but *dayum,* it was firm and round and her fingers itched to squeeze it. It was hard to resist a tight firm backside. He bent to pull a bottle of water from the little fridge, and she got a full view. He glanced back at her and held up a water bottle, but he'd seen her eyes on his ass, and he grinned.

She nodded to the water and quickly walked around the desk and sat in the recently vacated chair. Her heart thundered in her chest, and her throat was dry. Needing to change the direction of her thoughts, she focused on the computer and startled when he set the bottle of water on the desk and said, "Here you go." But there was humor in his voice, and she got the impression he was laughing at her. *Jerk.*

Relief swarmed through her when Chuck blasted through the door, and the smell of burgers and fries wafted to her ravenous stomach. The smile he bestowed on her was glorious. He seemed genuinely happy to see her, which eased the tension that had grown between her and Levi. Two weeks, she could do this.

"I didn't know for sure what you liked so I got you a cheeseburger and fries and pie." He set the bag on the edge of the desk and began pulling food out and setting it on top. "Got the same for you, Boss, and I got myself two double burgers and fries and pie."

Sage blinked as she took in the pile of food spread out on the desk. It was enough to feed an Army. The sheer size of the burgers was enough to feed her for three days. The mountain of fries spilling out of the boxed containers boggled her mind. Then, he opened the second bag and pulled out three enormous pieces of pumpkin pie, and her eyes glazed over. This was absurd; she'd leave here a hundred pounds heavier. The aroma alone added ten pounds to her ass. Too bad it didn't add it to her breasts; she'd always been small on top.

"Dig in, Sage," Chuck said just before chomping into one of his burgers. She glanced at Levi, who had picked up a burger and began eating. He was watching her, though, and Sage internally giggled as she thought she'd show him just how much of a tomboy she was. She grabbed a burger from the desk, unwrapped it and took the biggest bite she could, packing her cheeks so full she thought she must look like a hamster. As she chewed, she took another look his way and saw him grimace before popping a few fries into his mouth. She watched his lips as he chewed and wondered what they would feel like if she kissed him. Quickly changing her train of thought, she glanced out the window.

His raspy voice floated over her and gooseflesh rose on her arms. "As soon as we finish up, I've got the plat of the town square; we'll need to make a plan for the festival and how we're going to handle it schedule wise."

Chuck spoke with his mouth full of food, so the words were a bit muffled. "That's cool, Boss."

Sage simply nodded and wondered where these crazy feelings were coming from. She must be lonely or something. Her last relationship ended more than what, two years ago now? Yeah, that was probably it. She should look for a sexy guy in town and get laid. Maybe tomorrow.

L evi had watched as Sage walked up to the glass door and steeled himself to look anywhere but at her. Staring at his damned computer, he could still see her in his peripheral vision, but could give himself a minute to relax. She stirred something in him that he had no right feeling. He was her boss, and he didn't do relationships. This could turn into a mess of epic proportions.

He'd glanced her way as she shrugged out of her hoodie and hung it up. Though she wore a loose fitting t-shirt, he could see she was slender and firm. Her narrow waist gradually smoothed into slightly flared hips. He'd watched as the muscles in her back bunched and moved as she hung up her hoodie and he'd grown thick below the waist. The slight pulsing had caused him to grimace.

Then she stepped closer, and her scent wafted over to him, and his heart beat faster. Fresh from the shower was irresistible to him, and his mind instantly wandered to holding her in his arms and breathing in the powdery fresh scent until he knew he'd never forget it.

Mentally shaking himself from his musings, he

focused on his food and the tasks at hand. Biting into another French fry, he said, "I have a friend coming into town tomorrow who has security experience and will be helping us out during the festival."

Chuck's mouth was still overflowing with food as he tried talking. "Awesome. I'll have two experts to learn from."

Levi cocked his head and furrowed his brow a bit, and Chuck quickly added, "Well, you don't have a lot of time to teach me, so I can learn from Sage and your friend."

Sage chuckled and looked at him, waiting for his response. He still hadn't acknowledged her *expertise*, although he had to admit she'd been able to download the software and set up Mrs. James' system in short order today. He'd listened as he worked on the wiring and Sage had explained to Mrs. James how to access her control panel and how to monitor the system. She had a way about her when it came to explaining things to others. She patiently answered questions, even though she'd answered them before. They'd left Mrs. James' house with a plate of cookies, and Sage had received a hug and a kiss on the cheek for being so patient.

Levi quickly stood from his perch on the edge of the desk and walked to the wastebasket to toss his empty wrappers. He pulled the rolled up plat map from the top of the cabinet and unrolled it on the second desk. He listened as Sage and Chuck chattered, and she clicked away on his computer. He weighted the corners of the map with items from the desk: a stapler, the tape, a cup of pens, and a pair of scissors. The hairs on his arms stood as Sage's clean, fresh scent enveloped him, and her body heat mingled with his. He glanced into her eyes and saw they were seeking his. He clenched his jaw and looked down at the map and pointed, "This is the gazebo where there will be live performances." Moving his finger to a building marked *kissing booth*, he continued, "This will be a stand where hot cider and candied apples are served." Sliding his finger across the map, he stated, "This is the Hirschfield House, the townspeople turn it into a haunted house. I'm most concerned about this as it will be dark, people will be in costumes and with all the rooms, it will be impossible to track every room."

Sage stepped closer to look at the map and Levi stood upright to remove himself from her gravitational pull; his stomach roiled and flopped as he glanced at the shine on her hair from the overhead lights. The deep brown color was comforting, like a warm blanket and the varying dabs of reds and golds as the light kissed it, it reminded him of fine jewels. Her ponytail softly caressed her shoulder as it slid forward with the dip of her head. It looked like strands of silk, and his fingers twitched with the desire of feeling the softness wrap around them.

"That will be a problem." Her voice was soft as she was mostly talking to herself. Then as if remembering she wasn't alone, she looked into his eyes, "Maybe we could gain access ahead of time and install security cameras and monitor the activity from here."

Finally finishing his massive meal, Chuck stepped forward. "That's a great idea, Sage."

She looked at him and smiled, and once again, Levi felt robbed of her smile. She'd yet to bestow one of those on him, and oddly, he found himself craving it.

"I don't have that many in stock right now, and it takes a couple of weeks to get them here."

Her brows furrowed for just a moment and then a smile graced her soft lips as she turned it on him, causing his breath to whoosh from his lungs. "I know where we can rent some and get them here on time."

She pulled her cell phone from her back pocket and tapped the screen a few times. Holding the phone to her ear, she stepped away from the desk. Levi glanced at her backside as it wiggled and his cock stirred. He heard Chuck snicker and glanced at him only to see him watching his display of weakness. Levi grimaced again, and Chuck quickly diverted his attention back to the map.

"Hey, Dirks, do you still have that box of security cameras? How soon can you get them sent to Sapphire Falls, Nebraska?" She listened and then replied, "No, I'm here working for a couple of weeks, and we have a Halloween Festival where we're in charge of security. Need cameras to monitor a haunted house..."

She was resourceful; he'd give her that.

"You've got to be kidding me! How does that happen?" She turned and caught Levi's eyes with hers. She giggled, and his heart pounded in his chest. "No friggin' way! Sam McKenzie?" She raised her brows, and his jaw tightened. He nodded slightly at the question in her eyes. She continued her conversation. "Why don't you come with him?"

He glanced at his computer and saw that the screen was on and the bid he'd been working on was up. His brows furrowed, and he once again glanced at the little pixie in the room who seemed to have friends she could count on and a magic touch with computers.

When she turned, the smile on her face was breath-taking. "So, turns out my friend Dirks is in the security business with your friend McKenzie. Small world, right?"

It took him a moment to process her words. "What?"

"Dirks, my friend, served in Fallujah with your friend

McKenzie. I served with Dirks in Kandahar for two years and at Fort Hood for two years. They're just starting their own security firm in Kentucky."

"You fixed my computer?"

She cocked her head at the sudden change in conversation, "Yeah. That's what I was supposed to do, right?"

"She's good, isn't she, Boss?" Chuck's smile was large as he looked at Sage.

"Yeah. Good." He cleared his throat. "Let's get back to the plat maps."

He leaned down to the map again and let out a harsh breath when Sage stood across the desk instead of next to him.

8

The constant beeping annoyed the crap out of Sage, but she was too tired to do anything about it. As it grew louder and louder, it finally seeped into her sleep-fogged brain that it was the alarm on her phone. Reaching from under the cozy feather comforter, she felt for her phone on the side table, almost knocking it to the floor and pulled it under the covers and up to her face so she could see to tap it off. Heaving out a deep breath, she nuzzled her face into the still-fresh sheets and inhaled the clean scent. This place had the most amazing smelling bedding. She'd have to see if she could find out what laundry detergent they used so she could get it for herself when she settled somewhere. She'd sleep like a newborn if her bedding always smelled so fresh and clean.

She lay contentedly in her half-sleep state and listened to the sounds of the town. She'd worried it would be loud here, but it wasn't any worse than anywhere else. A motorcycle rode by, and the gooseflesh stood on her arms. There was just something about the sound of a motorcycle that got her going. She'd had one for a time while she was stationed at Fort Hood. It was cheap transportation and she enjoyed being able to ride when she wanted and for as long she wanted. But, then she was deployed, and she sold everything, so she didn't have to pay for storage or worry about it sitting somewhere. When she came back to the States, she had only the gear she could carry and her bank accounts. Now she was broke, still in a small town, and frustrated.

Taking a deep breath and throwing back the covers, she twisted and set her feet on the floor. She stood, and the smell of fresh coffee teased her nostrils, and her stomach rumbled. She grabbed her hoodie, glanced down at her clothing and shrugged. Sweatpants and a t-shirt would have to do. Softly stepping into the hallway, she heard low murmuring voices and followed the sound.

There were guests in the living room, reading magazines and chatting. Sage passed by the room and headed straight to the coffee area set up in the back, next to the kitchen. She could hear someone cooking in there, but until she was dressed properly, she preferred to stick to herself, get her coffee and wake up completely.

She prepared her coffee and quickly skittered back up the stairs to her bedroom to get ready for work.

Walking to the office, the morning air was crisp, and a light shimmer lay on the grass from the heavy dew. As she neared Scott's Sweets, the delicious aromas wafted out and called her in. Stepping into the quaint little shop, the sweet, warm air caused her to shiver. The smell of chocolate and coffee blended beautifully, and if she had thought she could have afforded it, she would have purchased one of everything. Instead, she settled on two truffles for each of them at the office, which grew to five today. Levi's friend, Sam, was arriving any time now, and her friend Dirks would be in this afternoon, since he was not able to catch a flight with Sam.

The blonde behind the counter smiled as she handed the little box of truffles over the glass case. Sage laid her money on the counter and inhaled the delicious aroma of the fresh chocolates. She waved goodbye and headed to work.

As she stepped into the office, the atmosphere crackled with a vibrancy that wasn't here yesterday. Chuck leaned against the second desk, a cup of coffee in his big mitt as he laughed at something. Levi—oh, my God—was sitting at his desk, leaning back in the chair, relaxed and laughing. It was beautiful. He had a bit of a dimple on his left cheek; his sandy blond-brown hair had been combed back, but a lock had fallen forward over his forehead and her fingers itched to touch it. She knew she was staring, but she couldn't stop. His smile completely transformed his face into a thing of sensuous perfection. The crinkles around his eyes gave him the appearance of a distinguished gentleman; his perfect smile made a lightning bolt zip through her body and land deep in her core. She felt her nipples pucker and was grateful she wore her hoodie again.

"Sage. Come in and meet Sam McKenzie." Chuck's warm greeting brought her back to reality as she turned her head and saw a tall, handsome man, with wavy dark hair curling around his collar and ears, leaning against the coffee cart. His dark eyes were a thing of beauty on their own. They positively sparkled.

He stepped forward and towered over her as he held his hand out. "Sage Reynolds. Dirks filled me in on some of your escapades together. I'm delighted to meet you and hope you'll do me a favor and give me some dirt on Dirks I can use as blackmail, should I need it."

"Well, that's going to depend on what he said about me first. You share and then I'll share. Deal?" The smile he bestowed on her was brilliant, and she felt like a lucky woman to be in the company of these three handsome men.

A phone rang, and they each turned toward Levi as he answered. Listening to one side of the conversation, they were quiet as they found a place against a desk or counter to wait for a debriefing of the call.

He ended his call and laid his phone on the desk. "Two more break-ins last night. That was TJ Bennett, and he's asked us to see if we can find out who's behind these break-ins. Last night a barn was broken into. This time, a water heater was taken from the Morton barn as well as a microwave and some food from the cabinet in the barn office. The other break-in was at a vacation house on the outskirts of town along the river. Canned food and some clothing were taken at that location. Luckily, no property damage, just stolen goods."

His gaze landed on her, and his jaw tensed. "The house on the river had a computer, and someone accessed the internet on it. You think you can take a look and see if you can tell what sites they were on?"

"Sure."

Sage watched him process his thoughts. "The cameras won't be here until around two o'clock." He turned his head to address Chuck and Sam. "You two can go on ahead to the haunted house and look at what we have in there. Make some diagrams and come up with a game plan, and then let's meet back here in time to meet Dirks. Got it?"

Sage processed what this meant. She'd be working with Levi today? She'd have to spend most of the day near him? She hadn't thought this was a possibility and suddenly her mouth was dry and her fingers twitched. The voices of the men faded away as she tried to get control of herself. Her heartbeat ramped up; the thundering of it pushing her blood through her system was deafening. She licked her lips and swallowed to moisten her parched throat.

"Sage?" She blinked and Levi came into view, his brows furrowed. "Anything wrong?"

"No, I was just thinking about some of the things I want to check on the computer." She slowly breathed in deep and let it out steadily to calm her raging heart.

His voice was measured, "Okay, let's get rolling."

9

"Do you want a truffle?"

Levi glanced away from the road and into Sage's dark brown eyes. They sparkled in the sunlight. As it streamed into the truck, it created a halo around her head, causing the natural highlights in her hair to glimmer. He pulled his eyes away from hers for a moment to check the road and then looked at the box in her hand. The top was open and inside were some truffles from Scott's Sweets—the aroma of dark chocolate swirled around the cab of the truck.

He reached into the box and lifted one of the chocolaty confections out and popped it into his mouth. He tried stifling the groan but was unsuccessful. He saw her smile from the corner of his eye as she reached into the box and pulled a treat out for herself. She bit into it and moaned loudly. "Oh my God, these are as good as they smell."

"Yes, they are. Why the treat?"

He found it difficult to concentrate on the road and

the task at hand with her so close. The sun heated the cab of his truck, which in turn heated their bodies. The shower soap she'd used that morning filled the cab, and his breathing accelerated. He tried remembering the last time he'd actually spent time with a woman, and the memory eluded him. It had been that long.

"I walked by the shop yesterday, and it smelled so good I made a note to stop this morning and pick up something tasty to snack on."

He turned his right signal on and navigated the corner.

Her voice was wistful. "What do you like about living here?" He glanced at Sage and saw her looking out the window at the passing houses.

"I don't know. It's fairly quiet. Peaceful. I've actually managed to be left alone for the most part."

She turned toward him. "You've been able to be left alone in a small town? How does that happen?"

He smiled at her tone. "I'll admit it takes some work. I go to the diner every morning for breakfast and let myself be seen enough that people aren't unusually curious. I chat up Viv, and she spreads the word about what's going on. The rest just leave me alone then."

She twisted her whole body to face him. "Isn't it backward to want to be left alone when you're trying to build a business?"

He chuckled, "You'd think so. But it's had just the opposite effect here. Plus, most of my clientele comes from the neighboring towns, so it works."

"Hmm," she said as she turned to face the front.

"Why don't you like small towns?"

"What makes you say that?"

"Chuck."

He watched her nod her head and grinned. There was a faint chocolate smudge on the corner of her lip, and he squeezed the steering wheel to keep his hands from reaching over and wiping it away.

When she spoke, it was soft, almost a whisper. "I'm from a small town, and I couldn't wait to leave it when I graduated. I find them stifling."

"Maybe you were living in the wrong one."

"I didn't have much of choice now, did I?" She sat back into the seat, and he was sorry he'd put the sadness back into her eyes. She'd looked sad most of yesterday when he'd seen her. Either that or mad, mostly at him. He'd been an ass to her, and he regretted it now.

"Guess not." He navigated another corner and cleared his throat. "You said you recently lost your father. Sorry for your loss."

Her lips formed a straight line, and he braced himself in case she broke out into tears.

"Thanks. He was sick for a long time. It was a blessing when he finally let go."

Admiring her fortitude, he pulled the truck into a driveway shaded by trees. As they reached the house, the beautiful view of the river below was stunning. The sun glinted off the water as it moved along its path, around rocks poking out here and there and then on downstream. She sat up straight, and her mouth fell slightly open at the sight before them.

She sighed, "Wow."

"That's what I was going to say."

"Whose house is this?"

"Mark and Janet Sommers. It's their vacation home."

"How did they find out someone had broken in?"

"They have a security system in place—not mine—and they accessed it last night when they got home."

"They weren't alerted on their phones?"

He shrugged, "Guess not."

She opened the door and dropped to her feet, and he sat transfixed at her gracefulness. She slowly walked toward the edge of the lawn before it dropped off into the river below. The slight breeze sent tendrils of hair in motion, swaying slightly. The hoodie she continued to wear hid her slender figure but her posture was straight, and he noticed that when she stood still, she was standing "at ease," supposedly casual but waiting for orders. She hadn't gotten out of the habit yet, still so in tune with military life. Of course, it could be that was a direct reaction to him; he'd not been overly welcome.

He stepped out of the truck and quietly closed the door, hating to disturb the serene picture she made.

He soundlessly moved alongside her and stared at the splendor around them. This was a perfect location for a home. His left a bit to be desired, though it was nice and quaint; but he'd done little to decorate or make it a home. The light covering of crimson leaves on the ground around the trees lent the landscape a magnificent cloak to shield it from the cooler nights.

Levi turned to enter the cabin, by using an entry code given to him by the homeowner. Opening the door, he stepped into the kitchen which he assumed had been immaculate when the homeowners left a couple of weeks ago, but now cabinet doors were left open, and various items had been dropped on the counters and left. Sage stepped into the room, and he watched as she took in her surroundings. Her eyes landed on each exit—the window, then doors—and he could almost see her calculating how much time it would take her to reach any of them should danger appear. He smirked at her habits.

He stepped farther into the room and located the computer at a little desk between the kitchen and dinette area. He bent and moved the mouse on the desk, and the screen came to life. Sage soon joined him at the desk and his heartbeat quickened at her nearness. She sat in the chair and began clicking and typing. Levi needed the space from her, so he wandered around the house inspecting the location of where the stolen items had come from. He snapped pictures with his phone as he moved from room to room. He heard the printer turn on and stepped back into the dinette area to see what Sage was printing. She glanced up at him and smiled.

"These were kids. They accessed the official Pokémon site, the Minecraft site, and one porn site. They didn't look for banking or credit card information, and they didn't try to purchase anything. But I'd still change my passwords—just in case."

"The police told them to change all of their passwords and monitor their credit scores for anything suspicious."

She pulled the printed documents from the printer and handed them to Levi. "These are the sites they accessed. I printed all of them and then deleted the cookies and browser history. I'm happy to run a virus scan while we're here."

He looked over the documents she'd printed and then glanced into her eyes. "This is very impressive, Sage."

She shrugged, "Thanks."

He continued to stare into her eyes, the deep brown color so dark and mysterious in the dim light of the cabin. His eyes dropped to the chocolate smudge still on her lips, and he reached forward and swiped it with the pad of this

thumb. Her skin felt like the softest satin, and she instinc-
tively licked her lip and swathed his thumb in her
warmth. His pulse quickened in time with the beating of
her heart, which was visible in the pulsing of her neck. He
leaned forward, hesitated, and then touched his lips to
hers, lightly, tenderly. When a little whimper sounded in
her throat, he clasped her head in his hands and deepened his kiss, mingling his tongue with hers. He stepped
into her body and his heart thundered in his chest. Then
she wrapped her arms around his waist, and he groaned.

Hearing a car door slam, he pulled away and stepped
back. The dazed look on her face was sexy as hell, and he
had to fight himself not to pull her into his arms and hold
her close to his body. Yeah, it'd been a long time since he'd
spent time with a woman, and this one had sparked his
interest.

The cabin door opened, and a short, balding man
stepped inside and flipped the light switch. He looked in
their direction and froze. Stepping forward, Levi held out
his hand and introduced himself.

The man replied, "Mark Sommers. How bad does it
look?"

"We think it was kids based on what they accessed on
your computer—games, no purchases, and no banking
information was accessed." He handed Sommers the
printouts and explained about the virus scan. "I spoke to
the police before we drove out here and they noted the
comments you made about what you thought was missing, but they didn't have anything further to go on. The
other robbery had a water heater stolen. That doesn't
seem like kids, so we'll have to compile all of our data and
see what they come up with."

Sommers looked around and swiped at his forehead. "What's all that black powder on the counters?"

"Fingerprint dusting. They didn't find any." He glanced at Sage and saw her rigid stance, hands behind her back, jaw tense, waiting for her next order. He reached over and patted her shoulder. "Relax."

10

Dazed and confused would be an apt description. Mr. Sommers walked in and all Sage could do was stand at ease and try to get her head around it all. He'd kissed her. He'd actually kissed her and it was...phenomenal. Her heart was still racing, the blood rushing through her body so loudly she couldn't hear the conversation between Levi and Mr. Sommers, and thankfully she didn't need to. Then, he touched her again, and she had to blink and swallow and try to clear her head.

"Relax."

Relax? He was kidding, right? Letting out a long-held breath, she widened her stance and brought her hands around the front of her body.

Mr. Sommers scratched his head and then said, "Why didn't my security system alert us to the fact that someone was in here? It's supposed to send a notification to our phones when there's an intrusion."

Well, this she knew. "Your system is a bit older, and the updates haven't been done in over a year." The puzzled look he gave her brought a smile to her lips. She pointed to the papers he was holding. "I checked while I was on your computer. Our company uses the G-eighteen, which is the newest on the market and a far superior system than the one you currently have. It auto updates, links via an app on your phone, which also includes video—not just an alert—but you can watch on your phone and see what's happening. It will simultaneously alert the police department. Once you get it installed, it's effortless."

Levi looked at her, and his eyebrows rose into his hairline. She swallowed and glanced at Mr. Sommers who slowly whistled and responded with, "Wow."

The pink tinted her cheeks as she gazed at Levi. He was still staring at her, and a small smile played upon his sexy, delicious, and oh-so-tender lips. Shaking her head slightly, she simply said, "What?"

He chuckled, "You really do know this system."

"Yeah, I said that." She crossed her arms in front of her and fisted her hands to stem the frustration she felt. He still didn't think she was capable.

Mr. Sommers heaved out a breath. "Okay, well I have to do a full inventory now that you and the police are finished here. Who should I give my final accounting to?"

"Give it to the police; they'll share with me if they need more assistance. The mayor asked me to help with the investigation, but I don't want to step on any toes."

Mr. Sommers glanced at her. "I'd like to hear more about that system you use; it appears it's time to upgrade."

"Of course. Just tell me what works for you."

They left the Sommers home, and Sage couldn't help stepping to the edge of the yard once more and taking in the movement of the water flowing below them. She watched the river meander around a bend and disappear.

She felt him before she heard or saw him. He was quiet, and she wasn't sure if he was nervous about kissing her or just always quiet. "Did you come from a small town, Levi?"

He let out a shallow breath, "Yeah. I grew up just outside of Lexington, Kentucky in a little town about the size of a postage stamp. My parents were farmers, and my aunts and uncles all lived within a five-mile radius. Those were good days. But, I've lived on one Army base or another for the past twenty-five years, and it seems a lifetime since I've lived in a small town until I came here."

She didn't know what to say. They had different childhoods, and hers wasn't all that happy. She had no real family to speak of and there was never enough money. Her father hopped from job to job always seeking something he couldn't find.

"Why didn't you go back home instead of coming here?"

He took a deep breath before answering. She turned slightly, and a puff of spicy scent floated from him, wafted in front of her, and it gave her gooseflesh. She glanced at his strong jaw; he stood proud and tall, his sandy hair tinted with silver strands that sparkled in the sun.

"I threw a dart at a map when I was leaving the Army. Most of my family is gone now. A few cousins here and there, but there's virtually no one left at home."

"Why did everyone leave if it was so great?"

He turned to look into her eyes and her breath hitched. "My father and his brothers and my mother's brothers were all military men. One by one we all joined one branch of the service or another and found our homes elsewhere."

"Is that where she lives?"

He turned to face her head on, his jaw tightened, he

straightened his back, and the look in his eyes told her she was way out of line. "I don't know who you've been talking to or what you've heard, but I don't talk about her."

She watched him stomp back to the truck, his limp now clearly evident and her heart thundered in her chest. She needed to shut her mouth and not ask so many questions. Just because he'd kissed her didn't mean she had the right to ask him personal questions. She shook her head, wistfully glanced back at the beauty below her, and trudged back to the truck, bracing herself for the tongue-lashing she felt she deserved.

Opening the door, she quietly climbed up and sat in the seat, pulling the seat belt across her body and fastening it. He started the truck without another word and backed them out of the driveway. Not sure what, if anything, she should say, she sat like a stone—heavy and silent until he spoke the first word.

They were almost back to town when his phone rang. He tapped the Bluetooth connector on the dash and said, "Jacobson."

"Hi, Levi; it's Ed. TJ says you're helping out with the investigation in the break-ins and I'd like you to come out to the Morton farm and see this mess out here. Are you somewhere close?"

"Yeah, I'm not far away. I'll be there in about five minutes."

"Thanks, Levi. I'm not used to investigating stuff like this. Appreciate it."

Levi tapped the disconnect button and finally spoke to her. "Ed is the local cop. There isn't a lot of crime around here, so this is a bit overwhelming for him."

"Then why did you want to start a security firm in a small town?"

"I'm doing well enough that I can pay you a small fortune to come in and help. I'm paying Chuck, and I've got more business than the three of us can handle."

He stared out the windshield and Sage winced at the tone. She didn't mean to turn things back so far.

Breathing a sigh of relief when he turned the truck into a driveway, Sage took in the surroundings and noted a prosperous farm—neatly painted buildings, barn, and a home. A cop car was parked in front of the barn, and the door was open. She could see two men walking around inside the barn.

Levi barely had the truck in park, and Sage had the door open and was ready to jump out. "Hey. Sorry I got so sarcastic. It was uncalled for."

Sage saluted him with two fingers and strode to the barn, needing the space so she could think.

11

L evi hesitated as he watched Sage march toward the barn, hands in the pockets of her gray hoodie, a small cloud of dust swirling around her boots as she tromped in the dusty drive up to the barn. Her head was held high, though, and he continued to wonder what it was about her that had him kissing her one minute and snapping at her the next.

He stepped out of the truck and winced when he put weight on his bum leg. Reaching back into the truck, he grabbed the bottle of anti-inflammatory, popped one into his mouth, swallowed it down without water, and headed to the barn to see what was up.

As he neared, he heard Tim Morton and Ed telling Sage about the festival.

Tim said, "It's the best time of the year here. On Saturday there's a paintball fight between the zombies and the zombie slayers out at Tucker Bennett's farm. It's a blast. Sunday, there's a DJ in the town square and a costume contest. Prizes are awarded for the best costume, and of course, the Haunted House is where all the fun stuff happens."

Ed chimed in. "By fun stuff, he means that's where our young girls lose their innocence, and more than a few babies have been conceived in that house." He shook his head.

"Well, I promise not to get pregnant in the haunted house, or anywhere else for that matter." She giggled, and his stomach flipped at the sound. It was like the sound of water bubbling along the rocks. Soothing.

Ed waved him in. "There he is. Come on in, Levi; leg giving you fits today?"

"Not any more than usual, Ed." Levi shook hands with both men. "Tim. I see you've met Sage."

Both men nodded and Ed began to explain the troubles. "So, here's where the water heater had been. It wasn't hooked up; Tim here, was going to put it in the milk house but didn't get the chance." Ed pointed to a corner where it was apparent a large object had been—the dust around the clean circle the only evidence. He then walked to a doorway. "In here..." They followed behind him. "There was a microwave on this shelf, and that's gone. Strangely, though, what's also missing is two boxes of cereal that were in this cabinet." He opened a door in the cabinet and pointed to where now was an empty space. "Even weirder..." Ed continued as he walked over to the desk and pulled open the top drawer, "there's a container of coins in here, not touched. A twenty-dollar bill and a watch." He stood and looked at Levi. "What do you make of all of that?"

Levi looked around the barn, then at Tim. "Do you know what time this all went missing, Tim?"

Tim shook his head and scratched the back of his

neck. "The closest I can tell is after one in the morning. I was up until then watching television. I always look out the windows before I go to bed, just as the last check. I didn't see anything or anyone around." He glanced at Sage and shrugged. "I was up around six this morning. That's when I noticed everything missing and called Ed."

Levi took a deep breath and then looked at Sage. "Thoughts?"

She shook her head. "It doesn't seem like the same people who robbed the Sommers' home. That, I'm sure, was kids. Food, clothing, and played on the computer. A water heater weighs, what? A hundred and fifty pounds or so? That's pretty heavy for kids to carry, not to mention bulky."

He watched her walk outside and look at the dirt in the driveway. She followed the driveway all the way to the end and then slowly walked back. She stopped and took a couple of pictures with her phone and then slowly glanced around at the grass. Snapping a few more pictures, she walked back into the barn.

"I don't see tire tracks of any note, but there are small tracks about an inch in diameter and about two feet apart in the middle of the driveway and then across the grass leading to that field over there." She pointed, and all three of them turned in that direction. Levi squinted, and sure enough, he could see what she was talking about.

He looked at Tim, "You have any little wagon or cart that you pull around here?"

Tim shook his head. "No. Nothing like that."

"Okay, we'll compile this data and get back to you. Thanks, Tim. Ed."

He shook hands with the men, and Sage did the same. He watched her smile at both of them and his gut twisted.

He waited for her to walk in front of him, and she only nodded once as she acknowledged him. For about the tenth time today, he felt bad about how he'd treated her. This was a terrible pattern he had going.

They climbed into the truck, and before he started it, he turned to her, "That was some nice work back there, Sage. You're very observant."

She snickered and glanced out the window. "You mean for a woman?"

"No...I didn't..." Well, hell, he deserved that one. "Never mind."

He started the truck and backed out of the driveway. The ride back to the office was quiet. He didn't know what to say to make it up to her for being such an ass.

12

The ride back to the office was quiet, and Sage was happy for the break in conversation. The man positively pissed her off. And then, in the next breath, he intrigued her. Hopefully, she'd be able to spend some time with Dirks and just chill; she certainly was not herself these days.

Levi pulled the truck to a stop in front of LJS, and without a word, she climbed out and strode toward the office. Turning the handle, her stomach dropped. The door was locked, which meant no Dirks, no Chuck, no Sam. Great, that also meant she'd be alone with Levi again; she so didn't want that.

She heard him walking slowly behind her and she stepped aside to let him unlock the door. Hearing him try to stifle the pain he must be feeling, she looked into his eyes. "What happened to your leg that it gives you such pain?"

His tone was short and clipped. "IED in Iraq."

She glanced down at the thicker sole on one shoe and back into his face which was tense, his jaw clenched. She wasn't sure if that was because he was in pain or because she asked. Being a little irritated with him anyway, she commented, "Good thing you didn't lose it."

He unlocked and pushed the door open, then stood back to let her enter first. "Says a person who didn't get blown up by an IED."

She entered the office and sat at the second desk. Shaking the mouse to wake up the computer, she watched him walk to the coffeepot and pull the pot of cold leftover coffee and pour it into the small sink at the back of the office, next to the bathroom. She began typing into the internet browser, trying to stay busy so the conversation would continue to be non-existent.

In just a minute the fresh aroma of hot coffee filled the room, and her stomach growled. Glancing at the clock on the computer, she saw that lunch had come and gone. Dirks would be here soon.

"Sage." She looked up and saw Levi had come to stand in front of her desk.

The door opened and in walked Dirks, rolling a suitcase through the door with a duffel slung over his shoulder. Sage jumped up and ran to greet her friend. He dropped his duffel just as she jumped into his arms. The hug was brotherly but felt so damn good. She needed this —a friend who knew who she was and what she was capable of. He set her on the floor, and they laughed together.

"It's so damn good to see you again." She smiled into his eyes.

"Damn girl, you still look great. I've been craving one of your hugs for a long time now."

She giggled like a little girl, the smile on her face so big it almost hurt. "You look great yourself." She stepped back and took in her friend. The smile on his face, the sparkling dark blue eyes, his short cropped blond hair. At only five-foot-eight, he carried himself like the man of larger build. He had a presence—always had.

"I can't believe you're here; it's so good to see a friendly face."

The smile on his face grew large. "I'm sure you met Sam this morning; he's a friendly face."

"I did meet him, but I don't know him. I don't know anyone around here. How about a drink later?"

"Roger that. I was lucky enough to get a room at the Rise & Shine, so we're almost roommates."

Dirks looked over her shoulder and nodded. He stepped around her and held his hand out to Levi. "Nice to meet you. Jeremy Dirks at your service."

"Levi Jacobson. Welcome aboard."

Welcome aboard? She'd not gotten so much as a 'no' when she walked into this office. Men! She watched Levi stand a bit taller but he seemed comfortable talking to her friend, and she had to fight the feelings of jealousy as she watched the scene before her.

"Have any issues hauling those cameras?" Dirks turned his easy smile on her.

"No, ma'am. I learned a while ago to travel with them in a suitcase and arrive at the airport very early to get through security checks. Helps to be ex-military; we get a couple of privileges here and there."

He grabbed the suitcase, and she moved over to the desk she had just vacated and pushed the stack of paperwork to the side to make room for the cameras. Dirks laid the suitcase on the top and unzipped it, revealing security cameras neatly tucked into little square, padded cubbies built into it. He pulled one from its resting place and held it up, winking first at her and then handing the camera to Levi for inspection.

Levi whistled. "This is a beauty. How on earth did you come by these cameras?"

Dirks glanced at Sage and smiled broadly, then swung his gaze back to Levi. "When we were at Fort Hood..." He motioned between himself and Sage. "I dated a little gal for a while whose daddy owned an electronics store. He let me browse through his ordering sites, and I got these little beauties at cost. Since I was getting such a great deal, I ordered twenty of them—just in case."

"Then the little shit broke his girlfriend's heart once he got the goods."

He laughed with her, and it felt good. She hadn't had a laugh in such a long time. Realizing now how long it'd been was sobering.

Chuck and Sam ambled in and loud greetings, introductions, and guffaws filled the room.

As the boisterousness died down, Sam looked at Levi and said, "We'd like to have a chat with you when you have a moment."

"Sure. Why don't we head on over to the local bar, the Come Again, and have a drink?"

Sage's stomach dropped. Her friend was finally here, and Levi was taking them away for "man talk." God, she was irritated with him. As if anything they needed to talk about was so above her head she wouldn't understand. She swallowed to keep herself from crying. Disappointment wasn't even a strong enough word, but no way was she going to let Levi know he upset her.

She turned to Chuck. "Looks like it's just you and me for lunch, big guy. You hungry?"

"Shit, Sage, I'm always hungry. I'll buy if you want to

go to the diner. The special today is roast beef and mashed potatoes."

"My favorite." She looked at Dirks, "See you later."

"We won't be long, Sage, just need about an hour or so."

She dismissed them all with a flash of the back of her hand over her shoulder which was meant to be a wave and a dismissal. She didn't want to hear it. Two weeks. If she looked on the bright side, it was now two days less than two weeks. She had this.

13

W alking into the Come Again, Levi scanned the bar for an empty table. He waved to the bartender, "Afternoon, Derek."

"Hey, Levi."

He found a table in the back of the room and settled himself in. His nerves were wound tight right now; the sad look on Sage's face as she turned to leave was like a punch in the gut. The second one in less than five minutes. The first was watching her excitement at Dirks' arrival and throwing herself into his arms. That hit him like a damned rock. He fought the little green monster that was growing in his stomach wondering what Dirks' relationship had been—or was—with Sage, and pissed at the fact that he'd be staying at the bed and breakfast with her. The thought that they might share a room made him want to bend her over a desk and leave his mark on her so she wouldn't want Dirks or anyone else.

Derek took their drink order, and Sam took the first opportunity to begin. "Levi, you already know that Dirks and I are opening our own security firm, but our proposition to you is to join us. I won't lie or beat around the bush; we need the capital you can provide. On top of that, you have the security knowledge and expertise we need. And mostly what you have is the knack for finding business."

Levi watched his friend's dark eyes search his face for a reaction. "Do you mean here, in Sapphire Falls?"

Sam looked at Dirks and then back to Levi. "No, back in Kentucky with us."

Dirks leaned his arms on the table and looked right into Levi's eyes. "We've got business lined up. We've got a friend helping us out with the basics in the start-up—the building, the initial capital to purchase computers and equipment, plus what we already have individually."

"Then what do you need me for?

Sam sat back in his chair, took a drink from the beer just set before him, then replied, "You're steady. Rock solid.

"So are you, Mac. Be real with me."

"I am being real. Here's how I see it working. You get the business and write up the bids. You've always been right on with that. We'll..." he motioned between them, "do the work. We'll do what you do here with the security systems, but we'll also offer surveillance, investigation, and computer forensics. In case you haven't noticed, Sage is a master on a computer."

Levi felt a jolt run through his chest. "Sage is joining you?"

Dirks chuckled, "We haven't asked her yet. I'm going to while I'm here. We've been planning this for some time, but until we had things more concrete, I didn't want to get her hopes up. She's always wanted her own firm, but I'm hoping partnering with us will be of interest to her."

"She doesn't seem to have any money. After fifteen years in the Army, she didn't save anything. How can she manage to own a business?"

Dirks cocked his head. "She had money, but her father wasn't one to keep or hold a job and didn't have anything saved for his last days. She spent almost everything she had to take care of him during his last few months of life and then she cleaned up his debts. He owed quite a bit of money to folks around their town, had hospital bills and no insurance, and he needed to be buried, which cost several thousand dollars."

Levi frowned and sat back in his chair. He hadn't even thought to ask, just assumed she wasn't good with money. His only close experience with women and money hadn't turned out so great. Jenny, his ex, blew through money like it was sugar. "I wasn't aware she'd been through so much."

Dirks sat back in his chair, and continued, "She's good people. Rock steady and one of the most reliable people I've ever met. Smart and not hard on the eyes."

Sam chuckled, "So, what other questions do you have, Levi?"

Levi looked into his friend's eyes and saw sincerity. He and Mac went back a long way, and when Levi had been hit with the IED, Mac was right there with him. He'd also been hit, but he was behind Levi and didn't take as hard of a hit as Levi had. Mac ended up with a nasty scar on his right leg, from knee to ankle, but that's it. No lasting pain or ill effects. "I've got to give this some thought. My business here is just getting rolling, and the thought of starting over again is daunting."

"It'll be different this time, Levi. We'll be in this together. We have a support network in place, we have the financial resources, we have the expertise, and we have a fair amount of business lined up. Back home, all those horse farms and stables use state-of-the-art security systems, and we have an in with our friend Lex's dad and his business partners. That's who's helping us. We're golden."

Levi looked between the two men. He hadn't thought about the horse ranchers and breeders. There was a fair amount of money in that part of the US, and it was a beautiful area to live in. And then there was Sage. Maybe they could use a bit more time to see what this attraction was. But Jenny was there too. He wasn't sure he was ready to see her.

"Give me some time to think about this, guys, and thanks for thinking of me."

14

Sage sat on the front porch steps of the Rise & Shine, elbows on her knees, beer in her hand. Her shoulders were tense; her gut had been upset since lunch. She shouldn't let this shit bother her, but it rankled that after all these years of working with men and having to prove herself, she was still having to prove herself in the civilian world. Dammit all, anyway.

"Hey, there you are." Dirks stepped out of the front door and sat next to her on the steps. "Got another one?" He asked, pointing to her beer.

She leaned back and flipped the top of the little cooler she'd purchased with her beer at Borcher's Liquor Store, just a couple of blocks over. She pulled out a beer and handed it to him. "Apparently the liquor store in town here sells some homemade liquor they call booze, in interesting flavors like watermelon and cherry. I guess it's tasty but can kick you in the ass. We'll have to give it a shot while you're here."

Dirks laughed, "Sounds like a plan."

She took another pull from her bottle, and Dirks softly asked, "How've you been, Sage?"

She looked him square in the eye. "I'm good."

"Be straight with me."

Her shoulders slumped. "I don't know, Dirks. I'm irritated most of the time. Pissed at the old man for putting me in this position. Starting over sucks balls, and I feel all alone in the world."

Dirks sucked back some of his beer and responded, "That's what I thought."

"Why'd you ask, then?"

He chuckled. "I like proving myself right."

She punched his shoulder, and they both laughed.

"So, Mac and I would like you to come and join us in the firm. You'd be our computer expert."

Sage had been drinking beer and coughed. Her eyes watered and Dirks patted her on the back a few times. "What? Why?"

"I just told you why. We need a computer expert, someone who can hack, set up systems, and offer forensic analysis on computers. Sage, we've got it all in place. It's going to be the best fucking firm in the country. We have major horse ranchers, and I mean major—the Saudis, the Irish—all of them waiting for us to get rolling and install their systems. This week's trip was to finish off our team. I was planning on coming to you anyway; it just worked out that you were here with Levi."

She turned her head so fast she got dizzy. "What does Levi have to do with your firm?

A grin spread across his face. "Whoa. What's going on with you and Levi?"

Her voice rose in pitch. "Nothing."

Dirks stared at her for a moment, his deep blue eyes

assessing hers. His grin turned into a full-fledged smile, and she could feel her cheeks flaming bright red. "Doesn't look like nothing."

She stood and walked down the steps to the grass below. "I just met him yesterday, and we kind of got off on a bad start." No need to tell him about the kiss; it was just a funky moment of weakness or something anyway.

"Then why's your face redder than the leaves in the trees?"

She took a deep breath and turned to face him. She didn't have any words, so she just shrugged. Then she thought a subject change would be good.

"So, did you guys ask Levi to join your firm?" Okay, so it wasn't a total subject change.

"Yes, that's what we wanted to talk to him about this afternoon."

"So if you're asking me, too, why wasn't I invited along with you guys today?"

"Aww, Sage, are you upset about that?"

"Yes. No." She rubbed her palm along her hip. "I guess a bit. Levi didn't want to hire me because I'm a woman, and he takes issue with women apparently. Got dumped or something and I guess it wasn't pretty so he doesn't like my gender."

"What? That's bull. Mac told me he's quite the ladies' man."

She didn't expect to hear that, and it tore into her gut just a bit. Stupid to feel jealous over someone she just met.

"I hadn't heard that little tidbit," she replied softly.

Dirks stood and grabbed two more beers from the cooler. He handed one to Sage and uncapped his. "Look, I don't know what's going on or isn't, but Mac said that Levi doesn't do relationships; however, he's definitely into the ladies." He sucked down some beer. "So, if you're thinking there might be something there, I wouldn't go with him."

She pressed her lips together and tried to tamp down the disappointment at hearing that Levi was a womanizer. "So, why do you want him in your business then?"

"One thing doesn't have anything to do with the other. But from what I hear, he's good at finding business, and he has a great head on his shoulders for putting the numbers together. He's the perfect partner for us to manage the office situation and keep business flowing in."

Sage looked out over the yard and down the quaint little street with its homes at the end and the colorful flowers growing in baskets on porches. White picket fences were more common than not, and it seemed that there wasn't a bad section of Sapphire Falls.

She took a deep breath. "I don't know, Dirks. I wanted to own my own firm on my own terms. I'll have to think about it, okay?"

He nodded. "Sure. I'll be here a couple of days. I'm helping you all out during the festival and you can ask me questions while I'm here. Plus, it will give us time to see if we can all work together."

15

Levi unlocked his office door, flipped on the lights and hung his jacket as Sam strolled in right behind him. "So, Viv has a thing for you. Have you gone out with her and then refused a second date, or is she looking for the first date?"

Shuffling to the coffeepot, Levi flipped it on and made his way to his desk. He looked at his friend. "I haven't gone out with her."

"Hmm, what's stopping you? Normally you'd have been all over her and several others by now."

He shook the mouse on his computer and waited for it to wake up. "I don't know, Mac. When I came here, I decided to be more selective, I guess. Small towns are gossip mills, and I didn't want to get a bad rep while trying to get my business off the ground."

Sam sat at the second desk, leaned back in the chair and grinned widely. "Is that right? So you haven't dated anyone since you've been here? It's been, what? Two years?"

"Why do you want to talk about this?"

"I'm curious; that's why."

The door opened, and Sage and Dirks walked in laughing. "And then you bet me five dollars I wouldn't do it."

Sage giggled. "Easiest five bucks I ever made." Dirks looked at the two men sitting at the desks. "Morning, fellas. Have a good night?"

Sam responded first. "Yep. Nice and mellow. What about you two?"

Dirks threw an arm around Sage's shoulders, "We pounded down a few beers and played cards with the other guests at the Rise & Shine."

Levi's gut twisted when Dirks put his arm around Sage. He watched her face for signs of something between them. They could be friends with benefits or something, and that rankled, too.

"Okay. We need to get the cameras in the haunted house today, then come back here and test the system. I have two new installs in York, and I have a shit ton of paperwork to do. Someone needs to take Chuck and help him out."

Dirks spoke up first. "Sage and I can install the cameras. She's a whiz on the system, so it makes the most sense."

Sage grinned at the praise, and her cheeks turned the most appealing shade of pink he'd ever seen. His heart-beat sped up at the thought of Dirks and Sage alone in a house together all day. It annoyed him, but he couldn't think of a thing to say to keep them from spending time together. He glanced at Mac and saw that the man was staring at him with a smirk on his face.

"Looks like I get Chuck. Where is he, by the way?"

Checking his watch, Levi replied, "He'll be here in a minute."

The need to move around a bit propelled him from his seat and over to the coffeepot. He had to fight to not let his limp show. The pain shooting through his leg was like glass sheering through bone. The shrapnel still embedded deep inside gave him pain constantly. The fact that his leg was now an inch shorter due to bone loss just irritated the piss out of him, but he tried acting like it didn't bother him. He poured himself a cup of coffee, and over his shoulder said, "The tools you'll need are in that closet right there." He pointed with his head. "The case at the bottom contains the cordless screwdriver and extra battery packs. I promised that no holes would be drilled into wood, so be careful."

"No worries; we know our stuff," Sage said as she opened the closet door and pulled the case out. Dirks grabbed the suitcase that held his cameras, which had spent the night alongside Levi's desk. He opened the front door and Sage walked out ahead of him. Levi's jaw clenched as he watched them walk to the SUV Dirks had rented. Each of them put their cases in the back and climbed into the vehicle. He turned to see Mac's giant grin. "What?"

"I'm thinking you aren't dating right now because someone else has caught your attention."

He plopped down into his desk chair. "Don't be ridiculous; I just met her a couple of days ago."

The door opened, and Chuck came in with the newspaper. "More robberies last night—two of them." He laid the paper on Levi's desk.

Picking it up, he began reading the article on the

robberies. Mac stood up and said, "It's you and me today, Chuck. We've got some systems to install."

Levi continued reading as they left. Food, clothing, diapers from a car in the driveway of a home and a farmer who said his garden had been cleaned out of all of his vegetables. Levi stood up and decided to talk to Sage about the newest cases. And maybe to see how she and Dirks worked together.

16

"I can see how this makes a great haunted house. Look at all of the rooms and places to hide." Sage glanced into the different rooms as they walked through the home.

Dirks took out his electronic notebook and tapped to open the screen he needed. "You said Levi uses the G-eighteen?"

Walking into the main living area, Sage was mesmerized by the old architecture and absently replied, "Yeah."

"Okay, I've got it, so let's go through and map out where each camera will go...starting in here."

They wandered through the rooms, Dirks noting on his touchpad the location of the cameras. Coming back to the living area, they began unpacking their hardware. Grabbing a handful of cameras, Dirks said, "Sage, I'm going upstairs to install these four cameras; you finish installing the cameras in here and the kitchen. I won't be gone long."

She pulled another camera from the case and climbed the ladder in the corner. Inserting the first screw on the base, holding it in place with one hand and the screwdriver with the other, she heard a floorboard creak. "I need a little help with this one in the corner. Can you help me?"

Having seen Levi coming up the walk from the window she stood in front of, she thought she'd play with him. She could have installed this camera on her own, but wanted to know how he'd handle this. He climbed three steps up the ladder behind her, and she said, "Hold the camera for me so I can get in underneath."

He wrapped his arm around her shoulder and held on to the camera. She tilted her head down and began screwing the camera base to the wall. His body heat enveloped her, and she shivered, not for the first time since she'd seen him. The man was simply sexy. She wondered if his body was firm and chiseled. She'd seen enough male bodies during her time in the service, so it wasn't that she hadn't seen nice ones, she just wondered about his. He leaned in and lightly kissed the bare skin just between her shoulder and her ear. She froze, and he nipped his way along her neck, eliciting gooseflesh on her skin. He kissed his way up to her ear, then slid his tongue around the shell. A lightning bolt ran through her body, zinging around until it landed between her legs. Her knees began shaking; her breathing grew choppy. "What are you doing?"

"Kissing your neck. Has it been that long?"

She whispered, "Yes." She shivered again, and he kissed the side of her face. She turned her head and kissed his lips. Light little nips. His breathing grew rugged and he whispered into her ear, "I couldn't resist."

She could hear his breathing accelerate and felt the shivers run through his body. The growing erection pressing into her ass was a good indicator of his excitement.

She said, "That's very nice. But we should get off the ladder; Levi could come in at any time and see us."

He jerked back and looked at her face. She tried to look serious, but it was difficult. She finally turned her head, looked into his eyes and giggled. "The look on your face was worth it."

He stepped down the three steps from the ladder and as she followed he slapped her on the ass. "Not funny."

Giggling again, "Very funny."

She stepped from the ladder, tucked her thumbs into her pockets and looked into his eyes. Her heartbeat increased, but she tried to seem casual. She cocked her head to the side, waiting to see what he would say.

He stepped forward, lifted her face with his fingers under her chin, and stared into her eyes. "You excite me for some reason; I can't figure out why."

His toffee-colored eyes searched hers, and try as she might, she couldn't look away. His scent surrounded her, the pure masculine spice that made a woman melt. She was melting into her panties right now—that was for sure. Her eyes landed on his full bottom lip, and she fought the craving that sped through her.

The boards on the stairs creaked, and Dirks' boots sounded in the hallway not far from them. Sage stepped back and turned to grab the ladder and move it to the next location.

"Hey, Levi, what brings you here?"

Levi pulled the newspaper from his jacket and held it up. "More robberies last night. Needless to say, the mayor would like this to stop; I wanted to see what Sage thought of this."

Sage stepped closer and pulled the newspaper from his hands. Opening to the news article she quickly scanned it, then handed it to Dirks. She watched him scan the article then looked up into Levi's handsome face. He was watching her, seeking her advice. The thrill that ran through her almost knocked her off her feet.

Dirks cleared his throat, "How many does this make now?"

Sage looked at her friend, "This makes seven now."

Levi's gaze never left hers, "What do you make of this one?"

"I don't know, but I think I'm going to have lunch at the diner and chat with Viv."

17

Walking through town, Sage took the opportunity to look around. She saw people standing on the sidewalk chatting. Kids jumped around and played games as their parents loaded groceries or visited with friends. Each store window looked clean and friendly. If she let herself think about life in a small town, this would be the perfect one. It was the polar opposite to the grungy town she'd come from. No jobs, dilapidated buildings, sadness everywhere you looked. Vastly different towns.

She stepped into the diner and the warmth circled her and instantly made her feel welcome. The aroma of fresh chili and breadsticks made her mouth water. She found a table toward the middle of the room and sat down. Pulling off her jacket, she tucked it behind her on the chair. Viv swung by and greeted her, "Hey, Sage. Glad you came in. What can I get you to drink while you look at the menu? Oh, and the chili is super good today."

Sage smiled. "I'll have a hot chocolate and a bowl of chili. And is that breadsticks I smell?"

"You know it is." Viv jotted into her notepad and scooted away, saying over her shoulder. "Be right back."

Sage glanced around the diner and noted that it was almost full. She pulled her phone from her pocket, swiped across the face and noted the time was one forty-eight. Full house and noon was here and gone. Many of the folks sitting in the diner were farmers, local business people, and there were a couple of truck drivers at the counter.

Viv floated back to her table and set her hot chocolate and chili on the table. "I'll bring your breadsticks around in a minute; they're still in the oven."

"Yum, fresh! I'll be spoiled."

"I'll do my best. So how do you like Sapphire Falls so far?"

Cupping her hands around her hot chocolate, she smiled at Viv. "All I've really done is work and sleep. But I was hoping you would take me around and introduce me to some of your friends."

Viv squealed, and Sage hunched her shoulders. Looking from the corner of her eyes, she checked to see what the other patrons were doing after that high-pitched noise. No one seemed to pay any attention; they must be used to Viv's antics.

"I'd love to. Ooh, we should start at the town square. The gypsy rolled into town this morning, and I heard her trailer is pretty special."

"Sounds perfect. Are you almost finished with your shift?"

A patron called Viv over, but before she left, she said, "I'll be ready to leave when you finish your lunch."

Sage waved her off, "Sounds good."

Feeling confident and thinking about what she hoped to accomplish today, Sage allowed her mind to wander to

Levi. He'd kissed her again and sought her counsel on the robberies. That was something. If what Dirks said was true, though, maybe he only wanted a quick roll in the hay. That'd be okay, too.

Then she mused about joining Dirks and Sam in their new firm. It could be a great way to get started in business, and it sounded like they'd gotten a lot of the legwork finished already, including some great clients. But she wanted to be her own boss. And working with friends could be like working with family; it wasn't always a good idea.

She ate as much of her chili as she could, enjoying every bite. Viv swung by, "Is that all you're going to eat?"

Sage grinned and rubbed her belly, "That's all there's room for."

"Okay, I'll box it up, and then I'm ready to go when you are."

They strode across the street to the town square and there it was, the gypsy's trailer. The authentic looking Vardo swathed in wood and topped with a metal roof sat under the biggest crimson oak tree in the square. The steps leading up were decorated with colorful votive candleholders, and multi-colored lantern lights lined the roof line above the door. It looked oddly out of place here and then again, not. She'd already envisioned the gypsy being dark and wearing colorful garb and scarves of every color.

"Oh my God, this is so exciting. I've never met a gypsy before. Have you?" Viv excitedly rambled.

Wonder in her voice, Sage replied, "I actually have, but it's been a long time. When I first went into the service, I visited Turkey on leave once, and I had my palm read."

Viv clapped her hands in excitement. "Oh, tell me all about it. Was she right?"

Sage stopped and turned to Viv. "She was. She said I had heartache in my near future, but I'd learn to move on. And she said I was going to suffer great loss, but it would be all right." She shrugged. "I had a boyfriend break up with me soon after, and I lost my father last year, but I lived through both."

Viv cocked her head, "I'm sorry, Sage. I hope this time is better."

She blew out a breath, "Me too."

The door to the trailer opened and a gorgeous young woman stepped from the trailer. She was wearing jeans and a t-shirt, just like Sage. Her long dark hair fell over her shoulders, and the shine that reflected from it was a sight to behold. Her dark eyes took in the two women standing and gawking at her trailer, and the smile that spread across her perfect face made Sage sigh.

"Good afternoon. You're here for a reading, no?" Her accent was undecipherable, but intriguing.

Viv tried stifling the squeal in her throat but did a poor job of it. "Yes, oh my God; yes please."

The dark beauty glanced at Sage but answered for her. "You as well, no? You're just shy."

Sage opened and closed her mouth, mesmerized by the woman before her. She cocked her head to the side as the woman slowly approached her, locking her gaze onto Sage's. "I will read your palm and tell your future. My name is Liz, and I have many gifts, but this is my best gift." She slowly took Sage's hand in hers and turned her palm face up. As Liz lightly traced the lines in Sage's palm, gooseflesh raised on her body.

"Hmm. You are interesting woman. You live in many

places. You have seen danger and death. You want a life different from what you have. And, ooh, you don't like the way you look. You hide in men's clothing."

Liz looked into Sage's eyes, the deep brown color so close to her own, but the exotic beauty standing before her seemed almost magical.

"I tell you this. I see inside of you, and you are beautiful. I also see a special man, but you are fighting it. If you want that different life, you need to be you."

Sage stood stock-still, trying to comprehend what this meant. Her heart thumped loudly in her chest, the scent of candles and spices floated to her and wrapped her in its warm embrace. She felt as though she were being snuggled into the warmest of blankets and a shiver raced through her body.

Liz turned Sage's hand palm down and lightly rubbed the skin on the back. "From this moment on, Sage, you have the chance to have all you've ever dreamed; you have only to open up and take it."

Liz squeezed her hand and then slowly let go. Sage instantly felt the emptiness of her touch but stood captivated by her as Liz read Viv's palm next.

18

Levi, Mac, Dirks, and Chuck walked to the town square to get a personal perspective on the area and how much space they were going to need to cover. Most of the activities throughout the weekend would be at one of the Bennett farms. Friday night a haunted hayride and hay bale maze at Travis Bennett's farm, and Saturday they were having a town wide paintball fight between the zombies and the zombie slayers at Tucker Bennett's farm. Sunday was the Monster Mash at the town square complete with costume contest and the haunted house. That was the day he was most concerned about. He hadn't been asked to provide any security for the other nights.

As they neared the square, he saw the Vardo trailer and Sage and Viv standing outside talking with a dark-haired woman. The dark woman seemed to be holding Sage's hand and speaking to her. Then she dropped Sage's hand and took Viv's hand. Sage stood motionless as she watched the two converse. She looked more relaxed than he'd seen her, and it was incredibly becoming.

A slap on the shoulder had his head jerking to the side. "For a man that isn't all that interested, you sure stare a lot." Mac walked past and set his canvas duffel on the ground. He immediately unzipped it and pulled his electronic pad from the side pouch. Tapping a few icons on the pad, he slowly turned three hundred sixty degrees and scanned the whole area. A beep sounded, and he tapped a couple more times and then turned it toward Levi, a huge smile on his face.

"This, my friend, is the kind of software we have to use." The device showed a picture of the entire park, including the trailer at the other side and every tree, shrub, and existing stand and building. Full color and the dimensions on the perimeter and with one more tap a perfect grid formed across the screen.

"This is just the beginning, Levi. You don't want to miss out on this stuff."

Levi grinned and couldn't resist taunting his friend just a bit. "Smoke and mirrors, bells and whistles do not a business make."

Dirks chuckled, and Chuck, ever the animated expression on his face, whispered in awe, "Wow."

"Hey, guys, whatcha' doin' here?" Viv's bubbly voice interrupted their banter.

Sam glanced at Viv in her jeans and tight fitting orange blouse, close to the color of her hair. "Just showing Levi the awesome software he could be using if he partnered up with us."

Sage leaned over and looked at the pad and then into Levi's eyes. "That's pretty cool."

"Is that a yes from you, Sage?" Dirks asked.

Sage smiled, "Haven't decided yet, Dirks. Still thinking."

Viv whined, "Levi, you can't leave here; we haven't gotten to properly get to know each other yet." She stepped to his side and added, "Maybe we could remedy that at the haunted hayride on Friday."

Levi's eyes darted to Sage's and the hurt he saw in them made his gut tighten. But she plastered on a fake smile and said, "That's a great idea. Sam, Dirks, and I can work while you have some fun." The sarcasm was there, just under the surface.

She turned and walked to the bed and breakfast without another word. Viv squealed, "It's all set, then; I'll see you Friday night at Travis's farm. Do you want me to pick you up?"

Feeling the jerk on his arm, he looked into the excited blue eyes of the vibrant woman in front of him and then shook his head slowly. "Ah, no. I'll meet you there, okay?"

She giggled and waved to the other guys as she strode toward home or somewhere else; he wasn't sure where she lived.

He glanced at the men standing around watching and then to Sage's retreating back, rigid and strong, her step almost gliding across the lawn.

"Way to go, Levi. You've gone and hurt my girl." Dirks' frown was pronounced on his face, but all Levi heard was, 'my girl.'

19

Veering off the road, Sage decided to at least make use of the remainder of her day and try and keep her mind off of Levi and Viv making out on the hayride. Her stomach twisted, and her heart hurt. They weren't an item; all they'd done was kiss a couple of times. Dirks was right about him—better she knows now than get her heart broken later.

She strode past the grocery store and saw a little boy around ten years old standing outside. She smiled as she neared him, "Hey there, just hanging out?"

"Yeah."

"You live close by?"

He looked into her eyes, "Not far."

Sage took in his clothing, clean but worn. "Where's your mom?"

He shrugged, "Inside."

"Not supposed to talk to strangers, right?"

He looked away from her eyes and down at the bag that held her chili. "Whatcha' got in there?"

She smiled, "Chili from the diner. I couldn't eat it all."

"Not supposed to waste food."

She shrugged, "Not wasting it. I'm staying at the bed and breakfast and don't have a fridge; you want it?"

He walked the two steps toward her and looked into the bag. The aroma wafted from the bag and his stomach growled. "Really?"

"Yep." She held the bag out, and he slowly took it as if she would pull it away.

An older boy, around fourteen, came out of the store and yelled, "Carl, what are you doing?"

Carl grabbed her bag and took off running, the older boy behind him. He ran around the side of the store and out of sight. Sage followed to the side of the building to make sure the boy wasn't in trouble, but neither boy was anywhere to be seen. She looked around her and didn't see anyone close by.

Shrugging her shoulders, she continued through town, stopping and chatting when she saw someone, just like she saw them all doing. She'd met a young mom and her two babies, one crying and the other on the verge. She met a younger man, around nineteen years old, a bit haggard looking and in bad need of a haircut. He seemed nervous and suspicious of her, so she moved on. She stopped and spoke to a bigger man and his teen son, the Carlsons. He was gruff, not overly friendly. "Haven't seen you around town, young lady. New here?"

Sage held her hand out in front of her and shook his rough, calloused hand. "Yep. Sage Reynolds."

"Oh, you're the gal working for LJS and staying at the bed and breakfast. Heard about you."

Sage cocked her head, "You have?"

He scratched his unshaven face, "Yep, had breakfast at the diner this morning."

Levi was right, go to the diner to be seen and talk to Viv.

"Okay, well I have to move on. Nice meeting you." Sage walked a few steps, stopped in front of a store and turned to see the Carlsons getting into a pickup truck, a water heater and some boxes in the back. She pulled out her phone and took a picture of the truck and the license plate.

Making her way to her home away from home, she skipped up the steps and uploaded her pictures into her computer. She wrote an email with the photos attached to Levi and Dirks asking if Levi knew them. She hit send, walked into the bathroom and began filling the tub for a long hot bath, and some much needed reflection on her day. She pulled a semi-cold beer from the cooler she'd carefully added ice to this morning and grabbed a pair of knit camo colored shorts and a green t-shirt. Setting them on the sink in the bathroom, she frowned. Liz was right; she did dress like a guy. She'd hung on to all her Army clothes and continued to wear them because frankly, she didn't have a 'style' like most women did. She'd worn little more than camouflage for the past fifteen years, only occasionally dressing for an event put on by the service or the weddings and funerals she'd attended. And then, black pants and a black shirt always worked. It was time to become a civilian again. The trouble was, how on earth did she go about doing that?

20

Levi and Sam entered his house from the garage. Sam headed straight to the refrigerator and pulled out two bottles of beer. Handing Levi one, he popped the top from his and took a long pull. Levi watched his friend down the better part of his beer. Once he'd come up for air, Sam took his bag back to the bedroom he was staying in. Levi took his own drink and stood in the patio doors and scrutinized his backyard. The trees were still beautiful, but the coating on the ground of fallen leaves was a sure sign there would be naked branches before long. Feeling restless and irked by Sam's irritation, he pulled the door of the dishwasher open and began putting away the clean dishes inside.

Sam sauntered back into the room, his voice terse, "Levi, Dirks really wants Sage to come and work with us. He tells me she's a great person, good on the computer, and she'll be good with customers."

Levi stood and faced his friend. "I believe all of that to be true."

"Then don't fuck it up. Did you see the look on her face when you made a date with Viv?"

"I didn't..." Taking a deep breath, he scrubbed his hand through his hair. "I didn't make a date with Viv; she sort of made it."

Sam crossed his arms in front of his body. "Did something happen between you and Sage?"

He huffed out a breath and assessed his friend's tense expression, "I kissed her. Twice."

"And then, what? You date someone else? Are you still skanking around with anything that walks?"

"No." Levi stomped toward the living room then turned to face Sam. "I haven't dated more than two or three women in the two years I've been here. And none of them from Sapphire Falls. No way to stay under the radar in this town."

Sam heaved out a deep breath. "So, you kissed Sage a couple of times, and that's it? Did you lead her to believe there would be more?"

"Shit, Sam, why the third degree?"

"Because, if she thinks you're an ass, she isn't going to come and work with us at the firm, not if you're there anyway. Then we lose out on a great partner and someone who brings a ton to the table because you've hurt her. You have to stop this, Levi. Jennifer has been gone for years. She's married to Tim; they have two kids, and it's over."

"Don't talk about her."

"Why not? You've kept her front and center all these years. You've fucked your way around the world, leaving broken hearts in every city you've ever been in for more than twenty minutes. Stop it. Move on. Live life. But for fuck's sake, don't fuck with my company and Sage."

Levi stared at his friend. His jaw clenched and his

stomach was in his throat. "First of all, I haven't fucked my way around the world. I've dated a bit. Second of all, I'm not fucking with Sage. I like her. There's something about her that intrigues me. And for the record, it appears that Dirks has designs on her; he called her his girl." It still rankled hearing that. He'd had it on replay since he'd left the park.

"As to Viv, I was dumbfounded at the square and didn't know what to say to her. I have no intention of going out with her."

Sam furrowed his brow. "What?" He rubbed his forehead with the pads of his fingers. "Dirks and Sage are like brother and sister. She's all alone in this world, Levi. She just buried her last family member after serving our country for fifteen years. Don't fuck with her."

Levi grabbed his beer and stomped outside to stalk around the backyard and calm down. His neck was so stiff, he thought he could snap it in two if he tried. His shoulders tightened, and his leg began to throb.

He flopped on a lawn chair and heard his phone chime with an incoming email. He pulled it from his pocket, swiped the screen and saw Sage Reynolds in his new emails. Taking a deep breath, he tapped her name to open it. Reading her comments about the Carlson's and looking at the pictures, he smiled. She was tenacious.

He riffled off a quick email back to her.

To: Sage Reynolds
From: Levi Jacobson
October 26, 2016 6:35 p.m.

. . .

I don't know the Carlsons and don't recognize the truck. Good work and thanks for continuing to pursue our criminals.

Levi

He finished his beer and stood to go back inside and apologize to Sam. Today sure had turned into a shit show in a hurry. He didn't mean for any of this to happen. Except for the kiss; he meant for that to happen, but he wasn't sure why. His head told him not to go there, but then he saw her and his knees weakened. And when he was close to her and could smell the fresh, clean scent that surrounded her, he lost all thoughts except for kissing her —touching her.

Now he had to figure out how to get out of his date with Viv without pissing her off. He didn't want to worry every time he went to eat breakfast that she was spitting in his coffee before bringing it to him.

Then he'd have to figure out how to make it up to Sage. And, more importantly, what they were together. Well, they weren't together, they were...working together. Probably not even friends. Since he'd met her, it was one misstep after another. He used to be smoother with the ladies. He was definitely losing his touch.

21

Newly bathed and feeling better, Sage made her way down the street to Julie's Apparel, the only clothing store in town. She hoped someone there would help her find something more feminine to wear while she was here, though she doubted there'd be enough of a variety to actually find her a *style*.

She opened the door to the store and was met with a medley of colors and styles hanging on racks throughout the store. She inwardly groaned, not being a great shopper and being on a budget. "Shit," she mumbled.

"Hey there. Welcome. Can I help you with something?" A voice called out.

Sage turned her head and looked around, finally seeing a little blonde head pop up over a clothing rack. "Hi. I could use some help picking out some clothes."

"Oh, okay." The little head was attached to a tiny little body. The young lady looked barely old enough to be out past dark, let alone working.

Smiling brightly, she stood before Sage, her long blonde hair pulled into a low ponytail, her bangs highly sprayed and probably wouldn't move if a hurricane blew in. "We don't have a huge selection here, but we have the basics—jeans, t-shirts, boots. Oh, we just got some super cute tops for fall in; come and look at these." She quickly strode to the table close to the register and pulled up a deep green long sleeve sweater with an asymmetrical hem falling past the hips. As she held it up, she said, "This will look smoking hot with your dark hair and eyes. Oh, and I have the perfect boots to go with it over here." She kept the sweater in her hand as she strode to the back of the store and pulled a pair of brown calf-high boots with a moderate heel and adorable buckles on the side. "Wear these with a pair of low cut jeans, and you'll rock his world."

Sage shook her head. "His?"

"Well, you're here because you want to impress a man. Right?"

Shaking her head no, Sage opened her mouth, but the little blonde giggled. "Don't deny it; I can see it on your face. Plus, your cheeks just turned bright red."

She shoved the clothes into Sage's arms and pointed to a dressing room in the back. "I'll pull a few more of our new things and bring them to you."

Nodding, Sage walked to the back and closed herself into the dressing room. Removing her clothing and trying on the first outfit, she turned to and fro in the mirror and admired the woman staring back at her. She pulled the hair band out, releasing the ponytail she so often wore. She pulled her long dark hair forward and was amazed at the difference the dark locks made to the intensity of her eyes.

The soft material of the deep green sweater hugged her lightly and made her feel soft and womanly. With the wide cowl neckline, her small breasts were camouflaged, which pleased her. She lifted her arm and pulled the tag from the sleeve to check the price. Affordable. Perfect.

"Here's a few more for you to try on." The clerk tossed three or four more tops across the top of the door. Sage glanced at the mixture of colors—orange, deep blue, red, and finally, an oatmeal color. She tried each of them on and had to admit they looked great. It was a good start to a new wardrobe.

She redressed herself, pulled the tops, jeans, and boots from the booth and stepped out to see Viv looking through the new fall tops. She turned, and her smile grew, "Hey, Sage. Looks like we had the same idea. I'm shopping for a new top for my date Friday night. What are you shopping for?"

Sage's stomach flopped and a queasy feeling fell over her at the thought of Levi with Viv. Actually, Levi with anyone else was hard to stomach. But, he clearly didn't feel the same, so she took a deep breath and responded, "I just felt like my wardrobe should look a little less military." She held up the tops she was purchasing. Though she wasn't going to buy them all, something about making sure she had the tops Viv was currently looking at gave her a little thrill.

"Oh, I love that blue one, I was just looking at it for myself." The smile began to fade on Viv's face, and Sage felt like shit. Viv hadn't done anything to her. Her shoulders dropped at the sadness in Viv's eyes, and she couldn't help herself. "Viv, if you are interested in this blue sweater, I won't buy it. Go ahead."

Viv perked up. "That's super of you, Sage, but I'll get this gold one. I think it'll go better with my hair anyway. What do you think?"

She held it up under her chin, and Sage nodded. "I think it looks lovely with your hair."

The smile Viv bestowed upon her was brilliant, and she had to admit, she felt better about taking the high road. "I'll see you later, Viv; I have to get a few more things and head back home. Busy few days coming up."

"I know. Oh, what did you think about what Liz said about my future?"

Sage's face paled, she could feel it. "I'm sorry, Viv. I guess I zoned out thinking about what she'd said to me." She held up the clothes she was purchasing and both women laughed.

"Right. Well, she said the man I thought I wanted wasn't the man I should be with, and that the man I should be with is right under my nose."

Sage cocked her head. "Hmm. What do you think of that?"

Viv walked to the register and laid her top on the counter. As she pulled her wallet from her large hobo bag, she said, "Well, I've been hinting to Levi that we go out for a while now and he hasn't taken me up on it. Today he absently said yes, but the more I think about it, the more I'm not sure he's all that interested. But, he's right here under my nose, so..." She turned to face Sage. "I guess I'm confused."

Sage giggled. "Yeah, that is confusing." The thrill that just ran through her at hearing that Viv didn't think Levi was all that interested in going out with her made Sage light-headed. "What are you going to do?"

Paying for the top, she tucked her credit card into her wallet and shook her head. "Not sure yet. I'm going to see what tomorrow brings and pray for clarity."

Viv grabbed her bag and waved to Sage and the clerk

as she left the store. "See you later, ladies; I've got some thinking to do."

Sage watched as the door closed behind Viv, turned to the clerk and said, "I think I need some makeup too, but to be honest, I've never used it. Can you help me?"

The little blonde squealed in delight. "Yes. Oh, this is going to be so fun." She ran around the counter to the makeup section and began pulling cosmetics from the shelves.

22

"Do you know who they are?" Sam put his breakfast dishes in the dishwasher and rinsed the sink.

"No. I've never seen the truck." Levi smiled at his friend, ever the neat freak cleaning up after them both.

Pulling his laptop case from the counter and slinging it over his shoulder, Sam asked, "Are you going to the diner to talk to Viv and see what she knows?"

Levi frowned. "No. Not today." He nervously pulled his jacket on and removed the keys from the little hook in the cabinet above the stove. "I still don't know how to deal with that situation."

Sam chuckled, "Chicken."

"Yep."

They each drove their vehicles to the office; they'd be going in different directions later on. Living just out of town and down a little lane gave Levi the solitude he wanted. After spending life on Army bases and in military towns, living among hundreds and thousands of people seemed incredibly unappealing when he'd gotten here. Now? He wasn't sure he was happy with his decision.

They each parked at the curb in front of the office. Levi opened the door and immediately hung up his jacket and began making coffee for the others when they got in. It also helped to work off some of the nervous energy about seeing Sage after yesterday. Damn, he had to stop being an ass. He'd tossed and turned all night thinking about how he'd hurt her. The look on her face and her retreating back haunted him well into the early morning. Trouble was, he didn't know how to fix it.

He flipped the switch to get the coffee brewing and walked to his desk. Sam had already set himself up at the second desk. He was tapping away on his laptop and seemed as if he was in his own world. Before he could sit, the door opened, and the lightning bolt that ran through him nearly knocked him to his feet.

Sage and Dirks walked in laughing. Dirks smirked at the look on his face and set a bag of pastries on the desk in front of him. Then he turned to Sam and said, "Look at our girl here; smoking hot, isn't she?"

Sam whistled and Sage blushed. She put her hands on her hips and replied, "Dirks, don't embarrass me. You promised."

"You shouldn't be embarrassed about what a fox you are."

She turned to the coffeepot and poured herself a cup of coffee. She was stunning. Her long hair which was usually tied up in a ponytail, flowed softly over her shoulders, the lights from above highlighting it perfectly. She wore a deep burnished orange sweater that dipped to a deep V in the front and had laces made of the same material, crisscrossed closing the expanse. The material looked soft and molded to her lean body in the most provocative way. The jeans she wore showed off her fine ass and shapely legs. The brown boots had side buckles, the heels giving her some height. And if that wasn't enough, she wore makeup which accented the almond-shaped, dark eyes he'd first noticed. Her lips were tinted with a light shade of copper and shined where the lights shown on them. She was utterly enticing.

She turned and looked at him for the first time since entering the room. She smiled, and his knees almost gave out. "Morning, Levi." Her voice floated over him like a fine dusting of powder.

"Morn..." He cleared his throat. "Morning. You look beautiful this morning."

Dirks walked over and nudged her with his elbow. "Told you."

"So what did you come up with where the Carlsons are concerned?" She looked into his eyes, and he had a difficult time looking away. It was almost as if she were a magnet and he was metal. Sam laughed and stood to grab a cup of coffee for himself. "You should see the look on your face. Priceless."

Sam stood in front of Sage, the large grin on his face almost Cheshire-like. "He doesn't know the Carlsons, and he hasn't asked any of the locals." He took a sip of his coffee, leaned into Sage an inch, and said, "He's chicken."

Sage's brows furrowed and she turned toward him, "What are you chicken of?"

He took a deep breath and let it out slowly. "Nothing. Never mind. Let's get to work."

Chuck walked into the office, stopped in front of Sage, and let out a long whistle. "Holy cow, Sage; you're hot."

She punched him in the shoulder lightly, "Don't tease

me or I won't teach you anything else about the G-eighteen."

Chuck held up his hands in surrender, "No teasing, I promise. You're killer." He said good morning to the others and turned to Levi. "What's going on today, Boss?"

Levi crossed his arms over his chest and said, "I need you to go to the diner and see if Viv knows anything about the Carlsons." He handed Chuck the pictures he'd printed out last night.

23

Sage dressed for work the following evening with a smile on her face. Levi stumbled over his words every time he saw her yesterday. If she didn't know better, she'd think she made him nervous. She and Dirks had laughed about it last night as they sat and had a few beers. But tonight was his date with Viv, and now Sage found herself not upset by that fact and hoping that what he realized was that she and Viv were opposites. Viv was flashy and vibrant. Sage was subdued and maybe even a bit broody. She liked computers and figuring things out, like these crimes around town and how they would handle security during the festivities, things like that. Viv was social, engaging, and bubbly.

There was no question he was attracted to her. But he just couldn't take that next step, so after his date with Viv tonight, Sage planned on stepping up for the both of them. In the meantime, she was going to find those damned burglars. She was going to stop in at the local bar everyone hung out in, the Come Again, and ask a few questions. Maybe she'd even meet some nice folks, and hopefully, she'd have a great time.

She exited the Rise & Shine and strode down the street. She felt stronger than she'd felt in months. She felt confident and, yes, sexy. She wore the soft green sweater she'd first tried on at Julie's and the cute boots and jeans. Her face was powdered and her lips shined. She wore the mascara like the gal at Julie's taught her, and she even managed a bit of eyeliner tonight, and it turned out decent the third time she'd applied it. Much better than yesterday's five tries.

She walked into the Come Again; the juke box was humming out a tune from one of Chris Stapleton's newest albums—her favorite of his, actually—and the buzzing from the talking and laughing in the full bar made her feel welcome. She found a spot at the bar and sat on the stool. The bartender came over, a big smile on his face, leaned on the rail and said, "You have ID?"

Sage laughed. "Really?" She reached into her purse and pulled her military ID from her wallet. She handed it over, a huge grin on her face, and watched his brows raise into his hairline, his mouth formed an 'O' and then he handed it back to her.

"You don't look thirty-three at all. What can I get you?"

Thinking she'd like to try some of the booze, she asked him for that.

"Sure, what flavor?"

She shrugged, and he continued, "We have strawberry, peach, and Mary just made a batch of spiced booze, which is great if you like spiced wine or spiced pumpkin pie."

"I'll have the spiced."

He walked away, and she looked around the bar. Most folks were coupled up, though there were a few groups of people. A group of men stood around the pool table and a smaller gathering of women sat at tables in the back. There were four couples on the dance floor swaying to the sultry tunes from the jukebox, and a bunch of men and women were laughing together at three tables pushed together next to the dance floor.

The bartender brought her the spiced booze and she took that moment to ask him some questions. "So, do you know anyone who lives around here with the last name Carlson?"

He scratched his temple, then said, "Yeah. Gus Carlson. Lives just out of town. Has three or four kids, I guess. Wife died about five years ago now." He watched her take her first sip of booze, chuckled, and handed her a tissue as the burning liquid slid down her throat, making her eyes water. "It gets better with each sip. But, sip is the key."

She dabbed at her eyes and nodded her head.

"You're not from around here."

She cocked her head. "That a question?"

He chuckled. "I guess a statement. How long have you been here?"

"Almost a week. I'm working for LJS for a couple of weeks."

"Oh, yeah. Sage, right?"

She laughed and shook her head. "Let me guess; you eat at the diner?"

"Well, yeah, but I found that out in here. People are always flapping their jaws in here. The more booze they drink, the looser their tongues get."

He floated off to refill drinks and chat with his other patrons, and Sage tried listening to the conversations around her. The couple sitting next to her were talking about a kid in school who'd gotten suspended again for the third time. Sad, she said, his momma was dying, and he was beginning to fail the tenth grade. Had a bunch of little brothers and sisters, too.

She turned on her stool and watched a couple at the table across from her. They were holding hands and talking as softly as they could over the noise.

She glanced around and saw the door open. Her heart sped up, and a heat raced through her body and settled in her core. He was here, and he was alone. She quickly glanced around again to see if Viv was here waiting for him. Maybe they'd decided to meet here first, but she didn't see the bubbly redhead. She glanced at the door again, and Levi wasn't there. Maybe it was the booze. Probably was the booze. She did another quick glance around the room and didn't see him anywhere.

"I see you're drinking the booze." She swung around and gazed into the toffee-colored eyes she'd begun dreaming about. His hair had been combed back, but that adorable lock fell on his forehead and curled just enough that her fingers twitched.

Softly she said, "Yeah." They stared into each other's eyes; she didn't know where to begin. So much for her bravado of being the one to take things to the next level.

"Hey, Levi; what'll ya have?"

"Hi, Derek. I'll have what she's having." The sound of his voice sent a thrill through her, and the scent of his freshly showered body and aftershave made her nipples pucker. He pulled out his wallet and set a twenty on the bar. She watched the muscles in his arms bunch and flex with the movement, and butterflies took flight in her tummy. She squirmed on her stool and looked into his face to see him watching her.

She swallowed, "I thought you had a date."

"It wasn't a date." His tone was clipped.

"Ah. Okay. Well, Viv thought it was a date; she even bought a new blouse for it."

Derek brought his booze and Levi leaned forward to pick up his glass, and the puff of scented air that circled her made her squirm again. She pressed her legs tightly together and then decided to cross them. That caused her to accidentally kick him in the knee, and instead of getting pissed, he chuckled.

"Well, that might be; but I didn't. And she's the one who called off my 'presence' at this evening's festivities."

Sage cocked her head and furrowed her brows. "She did?"

"Yes. I didn't quite understand her meaning and I didn't want to ask. She said something about someone being under her nose and someone who she thought she wanted to be with, or…I don't know. She was talking so fast I couldn't understand a damn thing."

Sage laughed out loud as she thought about Liz's predictions for Viv. "That makes sense."

He shook his head. "If it makes sense to you, it must be a woman thing."

24

He watched her face change when she laughed, and it was perfection. Her dark eyes sparkled, and the touch of makeup she wore accented the almond shape so perfectly. The gloss on her lips caught the light and drew his attention to the way they'd felt when he'd kissed her. He allowed his eyes to travel the length of her body. She'd crossed her legs before, and he had the distinct feeling that it was because he affected her in a sexual way. She sure affected him. The deep green sweater she wore hugged her body and accentuated her tiny waist and smaller breasts. He'd always found an over-abundance of breast on a woman unappealing—personal taste.

"So, your presence was called off, and you came to the bar to drown your sorrows?" Her voice took on a questioning tone, and he knew she was on a fishing expedition.

"No, I came here because Dirks said this is where you'd come. I stopped by the bed and breakfast first, looking for you."

She cocked her head, and the surprised look on her face made him inwardly groan. He'd sent her so many mixed signals it was a wonder she wanted to talk to him at all.

"You know, Levi, I don't want to be played with. If you think I'm just another notch on your very hacked up bedpost, you've got another thing coming."

He jerked back like she'd slapped him. Someone was talking to her. "Sam spreading rumors?"

She frowned. "Haven't spoken to Sam."

Levi took a big drink of his booze and immediately regretted the amount he'd just swallowed as the burn ignited a fire all the way down. Blinking back the tears in his eyes, he turned to face Sage. "Look, I know we've gotten off to a rough start. I came here to rectify that. I'm not looking for notches on my bedpost. I like you, Sage, really like you. I'm also incredibly attracted to you. I think you're attracted to me, as well. Also, we have to work together, and I'd like that to be successful, for both of us."

He reined himself in and took a breath. That was probably a bit long-winded. Oh, what the hell? He leaned into her and kissed her. When their lips touched, it was like an electric current running the length of his body. Gooseflesh rose on his arms as his lips slid across hers. The gloss she wore tasted like strawberries, the spicy taste of her tongue from the booze made for a sensual mixture. He raised his hand and held her head in place as he placed light little nips on her lips. Standing up, he looked into her eyes; his voice was husky from the desire coursing through him. "That's what I mean. That and I just want to be around you."

He watched as she opened and closed her mouth a couple of times, no words coming out. Her little pink tongue peeked out of her mouth and rewet her lips where his had just been. She bit her bottom lip as the emotions played across her face—excitement, fear, and arousal. They were all there.

Slowly she replied, "Okay."

Derek floated down to them, "You need more booze?"

The look on her face was fascinating, and Levi wanted more of that, so he nodded to Derek and held up his fingers as he said, "Two more."

"I've been able to drink and hold my own with the guys in the service, but this Borcher's Booze has a powerful kick to it and having more than two will surely knock me on my ass."

He laughed. "We'll go easy. I'm not used to it either."

Derek came back with two more glasses of booze and Levi chuckled. "Drink up."

He drank what was left in his first glass and watched her to see if she'd follow suit. The intention wasn't to get her drunk, just for both of them to relax. She picked up her booze and sipped, coughed once and then sipped again. She still had a bit left in the first glass. She giggled and rubbed her nose.

"It kind of makes my nose run."

He chuckled and looked into her eyes. The booze added a slight sheen to them. She smiled into his eyes and his cock twitched. Damn.

She turned to face him and looked into his eyes. "Are you leaving here to work with Sam and Dirks?"

"I haven't decided yet. My business here is just starting to thrive. I haven't heard an offer from them yet, other than partnership, that's better than what I have here."

She coughed on her booze. "Partnership?"

"Isn't that what they offered you?"

She set her glass on the bar and shook her head. She tucked her deep brown strands behind her ear and swallowed.

"Did you accept the offer to work with them?"

He watched her chest rise and fall. The music turned to another slow country song, and he wanted to lighten the mood. "Dance with me?"

She tilted her head slightly and hesitated. He leaned forward and took her hand in his. "Come on."

He pulled her to her feet, easily a foot shorter than he was, but with heels on, her head came to just above his breast line. He escorted her to the dance floor, and they blended in with the other couples. He pulled her close, tucking her tightly against his body, enjoying the feel of her curves, the smell of her hair, the softness of her body. He spun her slowly around and she laughed and looked up into his face; the thickness beginning to grow in his jeans hit hyper speed. His hand floated to her lower back and pulled her in tight, and she let out a soft breath when their bodies met. Her hands traveled up his shoulders and around his neck, and she tucked her face under his chin. He laid his head on hers and closed his eyes. They were no longer dancing, simply swaying to the melodic strains swirling around them. The couples around them were whispering sweet nothings to each other, the soft voices added to the intimate feel. Levi swallowed once, then twice. He hadn't felt like this since...her—Jenny.

He started to pull away, but she held on and mumbled. "The song isn't over yet."

He hesitated and it caused her to trip. She looked up at him, her brows furrowed. "What's wrong?"

His voice was gruff. "Nothing."

She withdrew her arms, and he instantly regretted

making her feel like getting away from him. He leaned down and whispered, "Nothing. It's okay."

He pulled her into him again, but the spell had been broken. Dammit to hell, he hated that. Hated it more now than ever before. Sam was right; he needed to let go.

The music ended, and Sage quickly drew away and began walking to the bar. He silently followed her and whispered into her ear, "Let's take our booze to go."

She shrugged, but said nothing. Levi held up his hand to get Derek's attention. "We'd like plastic cups, please."

Derek nodded and pulled two cups from under the bar. Setting them down in front of them, he grinned. "Thanks for coming in. You two have a great rest of your evening."

Levi nodded and poured their booze into the cups they'd been given. He swiped his change from the bar and held her cup out. She gently took the offered drink and turned toward the door.

As they stepped outside he breathed deep of the crisp, fresh air, the slight breeze just enough to keep them moving to avoid a chill but bringing with it aromas from the restaurant, local fireplaces, and those camping around the town square.

"It's nice out. Should we walk?" she asked. A small smile played on her lips. "My hometown is nothing like this place. It isn't clean or friendly or prosperous."

"I can see why you have a bad taste in your mouth for small towns then."

She took a deep breath, "I suppose we're both damaged by different things then. You can't hold a woman in your arms without being wary and hurt."

"Not true."

She stopped and turned toward him. "It is. You just

don't want to admit it." She began walking again, "Damned male pride. It's stupid. It's also unhealthy."

He watched her take a few steps away from him and shook his head. Quickening his stride, he caught up to her and caught her hand. Pulling her to a stop, he faced her. "Okay, let's do this again." He took a deep breath. "You're right. I'm trying." A dim light caught her eyes, and they seemed to twinkle at him. He kissed her lightly and turned them to walk again. "Help me try."

She squeezed his hand, "Deal."

After a few steps, he chuckled. "Your place or mine?"

She burst out laughing, and his heart instantly felt lighter.

25

"Well, I have a private room and a squeaky bed. What do you have?"

Walking to the bar tonight, Sage had hoped for a few leads on their criminals. She never expected that Levi would walk in the bar and she'd never have dreamed she'd be walking home with him now. But it felt right somehow, and she hoped this night changed their relationship with each other, for the good. He said he was trying and she'd cut him some slack. After all, she wasn't perfect by any means and she'd spent enough time with men to kind of *get* them, if you could ever get a man.

"I have a quiet bed, a private room, and a house guest."

She giggled, "My place."

Glancing up into his face, the butterflies took flight as his toffee-colored eyes gazed into hers. The warmth of his hand in hers and the chill of the night air sent a shiver racing through her body. The thought of being in his arms again sent a thrill racing through her body and landing in her core. The dampness gathering between her legs made her nipples pucker, and she fought the urge to run. They turned the corner onto her street, and a little boy ran across the street in front of them.

"Hey, that's the kid I gave my leftover lunch to yesterday," she startled.

"Why did you do that?"

"He looked at my bag, and I heard his stomach rumble; the poor kid seemed so hungry, and I don't have a refrigerator in my room, so I gave it to him."

The kid stopped behind a tree and peeked around at them.

She yelled, "Hey, come over here and talk to me."

He didn't move, but the rustling of someone walking through the leaves across from the boy caught their attention. Another boy, a bit older, ran around the back of a house and Levi stepped closer to the fence of that house, craning his neck to see something.

The leaves rustled behind them, and she turned in time to see the boy dash off toward the square.

"It's a little late for boys so young to be running around town, isn't it?" she questioned.

"That's what I was thinking." He looked around the house and then turned toward her. "Well, it's not like they were doing anything wrong. Not that we could see anyway."

He took her hand once again, and they continued walking to the bed and breakfast. As they walked up the steps, she looked back at him and held her forefinger to her lips. She pointed to a door at the top and to the left of the staircase. She mouthed, "Dirks." At the top of the steps, she turned to the right and led him to the end of the short hallway. She unlocked her door, and they slipped inside. She took two steps in, set her cup of booze on the dresser; he followed suit. She turned, he scooped her up into his arms and spun her around. She wrapped her arms around his neck and leaned down to kiss his lips. He stopped spinning and laid down on the bed, with her on top of him. The bed squeaked, and they both laughed. He held her head between his hands and kissed her deeply. She whimpered, and unable to control herself, she ground herself against him, thrilled when she felt the rigid length beneath his jeans.

She quickly sat up and began unbuttoning his shirt, while he reached up under her sweater and swiped his thumbs over her breasts. She stilled and stared into his eyes, her heart beating wildly in her chest.

"I'm not very..." She swallowed. "I'm not well-endowed." Her cheeks burned bright red, but she searched his eyes, waiting for the disappointment to set in.

"I think you're perfect," he continued to gaze into her eyes, "just the way you are."

Swallowing, she whispered, "You haven't seen all of me yet."

He tugged at her sweater, "Then let's get on with it."

She raised her brows, and pulled her arms from her sweater and then pulled it up and over her head. His eyes landed on her right arm and the full sleeve of tattoos she wore. Colorful red roses shaded to showcase the depth of colors and hues befitting the flower, tied together with scrolls of varying widths and leaves in deep shades of greens. His forefinger traced the flowers from her shoulder down to her wrist.

His voice was gruff when he spoke. "What does this mean to you?"

Wistfully, she explained, "My mom loved red roses. She died four years ago of cancer. I had this done as a tribute to her. And..." She turned her wrist outward and pointed to a series of small scars along the inside of her arm up to her pit. "I wanted to hide these." She looked into his eyes. "Shrapnel scars. IED in Afghanistan."

He heaved out a deep breath. "I can beat those."

She slid off to the side, and he unbuckled and unzipped his jeans. He lifted his rear and shoved them over his hips. He kicked them to the floor, lifted his right leg, pulled down the sock and showed her his scars.

His leg was mottled with scarred skin. Some of it looked like it had burned and melted, leaving a labyrinth of lines and marks. The scarring ran from his knee to his ankle. She lightly touched his dimpled skin with her fingertips, the smoothness a direct contrast to the rough ridges and lines.

"IED?" she questioned.

He nodded. "Ten years ago. Lost so much of my bone, my leg is an inch shorter than the other."

She slowly looked away from his leg and into his eyes. Hers had misted up; she knew just how much pain he'd gone through. She'd seen it over and over again during her time in service. "We're perfect for each other."

He rolled her over and covered her with his body. "Let's see just how perfect."

His tongue explored her mouth, the taste of the booze still lightly on his tongue, his scent surrounding them, his strength exciting as hell. He leaned on one arm and helped her unbutton and unzip her jeans and she shimmied them down as he unhooked her bra. After she'd dropped her jeans to the floor, he pulled her back down and immediately covered a breast with his mouth, flicking her taut nipple with his tongue, while massaging the other. She dug her hands into his hair and marveled at the softness of it on her fingers. He kissed his way down her abdomen, circling her clit with his tongue and sucking in.

She moaned as she spread her legs open for him and he immediately slipped a finger inside. She sucked in a breath, and fisted his hair, holding him right there. Alternating between flicking her clit and sucking it in, she exploded so fast she saw bright lights shooting behind her eyelids.

Hazy, she felt him climb up her body, placing soft wet kisses as he moved along. Swathing each breast in warmth, he alternated between them, kissing and sucking each hard nipple. The squeaking bed brought her attention to their location, and she opened her eyes and looked into his. He grinned, one side of his mouth higher than the other. He quickly stood and pulled her up with him. He leaned her against the wall, wrapped one of her legs over his arm, and thrust up into her in one swift move.

She groaned at the same time as he, and she reveled in his jerking breaths, his shaking body pushed tightly against her and the thrusts as his cock entered her, pulled out and then thrust back in. His movements were fluid. Her skin became heated and damp as they clung together, dancing the oldest dance of all time, perfectly in sync with each other. Her breathing came in short spurts as she felt her body flush and every nerve ending surged to where they were melded together. Every thrust sent new sensations throughout her body. She held on to his shoulders, her arms wrapped around his neck. As their bodies heated, the muskiness circled them, creating a whole new scent of the two of them combined.

Gruffly he said into her ear, "You're so beautiful, vibrant, and you feel so fucking fantastic sucking me in." He groaned, and the vibrations shot straight to her pussy, and she tumbled over the edge. He thrust once more and growled into her neck as his body tensed, his arms circling her tighter.

They stood, each catching their breath. He slowly pulled her with him as he stepped backward two steps and softly laid back onto the bed, holding her tightly. Short puffs of air close to her ear sent a little thrill through her to know she'd worked him up.

26

The sunlight streamed in through the split in the curtain landing across his face. He squinted his eyes open and reached for his phone: six forty-two. He had to run home and grab some clean clothes. He wasn't sure if he could go to the diner for breakfast and he didn't want to leave Sage. She lay snuggled into his side, her perky breasts firmly pushed into him. She stretched her legs against his, wrapped one over the top and nuzzled in closer. Inhaling deeply, she ran her hand over his chest. "You smell good." She sighed. "And I love chest hair." She rubbed his chest and teased some of the hairs with her fingers.

He chuckled and kissed the top of her head. Breathing deeply, he said, "You smell good, too." He smiled and continued, "I prefer a chest without hair."

Her sleepy giggle made the butterflies come to life in his stomach. He kissed the top of her head again and moved to get out of bed. He sat up and twisted to set his feet on the floor. Looking around for his clothing, he saw a sock on the floor at the foot of the bed. He stood and

waited for the circulation in his leg to kick in and the pain
to subside. His first couple of steps were rough; it was that
way every morning.

"Do you take anything for the pain?"

He turned, and Sage was sitting up, the sheet tucked
under her arms, but her nipples were taut and strained
against the soft cotton. His cock twitched and a slow smile
spread across her face. She dropped the sheet and crawled
like a seductive panther to the end of the bed, raised up
on her knees and reached for him. He walked into her
arms, enjoying the feel of her skin pressed against his. His
arms encircled her and pulled her tightly to him, one
hand floated down her back and grabbed a handful of her
toned ass, gently squeezing and then pulled her into his
thick length. His mouth sought hers and claimed it,
enjoying the way she tasted first thing in the morning.

A cell phone rang and persisted in being answered.
Levi pulled away from her mouth and leaned his forehead
against hers. "I have to get that. It's TJ's ring."

Walking to the nightstand, he answered on the fifth
ring. "Jacobson."

He listened to the mayor explain about another set of
robberies last night. When the name of the street was
mentioned, his blood ran cold.

"Yes, I'll be right there."

He hung up his phone and quickly went to pull on his
clothing, finding the pieces strewn around the floor.

"I could use you at another crime scene, Sage. It seems
as though there were two robberies on Fuchsia Street last
night."

Sage sat on her heels and cocked her head and
furrowed her brows. "That's this street." Her voice held
disbelief.

"Yes."

She slid from the bed and began picking up her discarded clothing. She pulled clean underwear from a drawer and a clean, long-sleeved t-shirt from another. She dressed quickly, and as she pulled a clean pair of jeans from the closet, she stopped abruptly and turned to face him. "Those boys we saw last night. I'm getting that funny feeling."

He zipped his jeans. "Yeah."

She pulled her t-shirt over her head. "Shit."

He absently watched as she ran to the bathroom and brushed her teeth, raked a brush through her hair, applied deodorant and dashed back to the bedroom.

"That was fast," he said, looking down at his phone.

"Fifteen years in the Army."

"Right." He walked to the bathroom, and pulled the door to, but not closed. He used the toilet and washed his hands. Seeing her toothbrush on the counter, he shrugged and used her toothbrush. She buckled the last buckle on her boot and smiled at him as he walked into the bedroom.

She stood, "Ready? We can grab a cup of coffee downstairs." She grabbed her hoodie and keys, slid her cell phone into her back pocket, and opened the door. He followed her to the hallway, glancing briefly at Dirks' door as they went downstairs.

Grabbing their coffee, they walked down the street, retracing their path as they went. Sage pulled her phone from her back pocket and tapped it a few times. Spreading her fingers on the screen to enlarge it, she glanced over at the place where the first little boy had hidden from them last night. She looked both ways and crossed the street, checking behind the tree he'd hidden behind and then snapped a few pictures. He watched her, both impressed at her skill and enamored with her being. He needed to be careful, or he'd fall in love with her. She was different in so many ways—mature, strong, independent. She didn't get all freaked out at his leg. She'd been there herself. They shared their military service. Now, they shared this. This love of a puzzle that needed to be solved. This energy derived from searching, hunting, and pulling the information from small things. He was screwed with this woman.

She walked back to him and smiled. She pointed to the other clump of trees where the other boy had run, and he held his hand out for her to pass by. She was like a dog finding a bone, hot on the trail.

He glanced toward the house just two homes away, where the police car currently sat. A quick look at Sage and he knew she'd figure out where he'd gone, so he silently walked the sidewalk, looking for clues along the way.

He tapped on the doorframe of the open door and Ed, the town cop, glanced up from his report. Ed waved him in, "Levi, thanks for coming down."

He walked farther into the living room of the house and shook Ed's hand. "What's missing?"

"The owner, Ms. Tisch, is in the back looking around for other missing items. A window was broken in the kitchen, the lock turned, and the burglar entered through the then-opened window. Ms. Tisch was away for the night, staying with her sister in Omaha."

"Okay. Have you dusted for prints?"

"Yes. There were a few on the window and sill. Nothing else in the kitchen. It doesn't appear that anything in any other room but the kitchen has been touched."

Sage entered the house, "Hi, Ed."

"Sage. Good morning. Thanks for coming down." He looked at his report and then at him and Sage. "Cereal was taken from the kitchen cupboard. She had a partial and an unopened box, both gone. A bag of flour, baking soda, some canned goods."

Sage asked, "Some eggs? Also chocolate chips and some nuts."

Ed looked up at her, wonder in his eyes. "Ms. Tisch didn't say anything about those items."

"I found evidence of them outside. Can you ask her to check, please? Also, does she have a computer here?" She continued in full detective mode.

Ed nodded and walked to a back bedroom; he could hear them chatting. Sage looked up at him and smiled. "How are you doing this morning?" Her voice took on a husky tone, and he found himself instantly turned on.

"I've never been better." He leaned in and whispered in her ear, "I enjoyed myself last night. Hard not to relive it in my head over and over. You're a sexy woman, Sage."

She smiled and blushed, the rosy glow in her cheeks immensely sexy. "Thanks. You're incredibly sexy yourself, Levi." She stood on her toes and pecked his lips lightly.

Ed cleared his throat, smirked, and said, "Ms. Tisch is having a tough time back there. Apparently, she had a couple of expensive outfits taken, her favorite jogging suit and some slippers were missing."

Sage looked around the room and saw a roll top desk. She pointed, "Computer?"

"Oh, yes, she said she has a computer in there, and she always shuts it down when she's leaving."

Sage pulled up the top of the desk and sat in the chair. She swept her long dark hair from her shoulders and looked enticing. She shook the mouse and the computer came to life. She turned her head and winked at him, and it shot straight to his groin.

She began tapping away on the keyboard, and he took that moment to check in the kitchen. He snapped some photos and glanced around. He walked back to Sage and kissed her on top of her head. "I have to walk over to the bar and grab my truck. My work stuff's in it. I'll be right back."

27

She smiled to herself as she watched him step out of the house. He was a sexy man, and she was fortunate to find him. Funny how things worked out sometimes.

She tapped through a few screens on the computer and found the sites that had most recently been accessed. She checked the favorites bar and then stood and addressed Ed. "Do you think Ms. Tisch will be able to come out here and speak with me or should I go and see her?"

"She's coming out; she just needed to blow her nose and touch up her eyes a bit."

"I'm here." A tiny lady walked down the hallway toward them, her short white hair neatly styled, and she wore a soft pink stylish jogging suit. She held out her hand, and Sage took it in hers. The frail looking woman had a strong grip, belying her tiny stature. "I've never dealt with anything like this in my life, and I have to say, it's a bit overwhelming."

"I'm sure it is, and I'm so very sorry you're going through this. But we're going to help you."

"Thank you, dear."

Levi walked back into the house and introduced himself. Sage had to catch her breath looking at the handsome man before her. He leaned down to speak with Ms. Tisch, his genuine smile wide, his demeanor warm. Ms. Tisch, clearly enamored by him, smiled brightly and even blushed a little. Sage completely understood that. He held his hand out to the sofa and invited the tiny woman to sit with him and chat, totally sexy in how he treated women. She had to rethink her initial response to him and thinking he hated women. He'd been distrustful of them, but maybe he honestly was trying.

"Sage, please tell Ms. Tisch what you found on her computer."

She looked into his eyes and saw the sincerity and even a bit of humor in his eyes. "Of course. It appears your computer was accessed Ms. Tisch unless you've been logging on to gaming sites and a bit of porn." She looked at the shocked look on Ms. Tisch's face, and the blush that tinted her alabaster cheeks. "Sorry, but I'm still of the opinion that these are kids breaking into homes. They take food; they play a few games on the computers, and they take clothing. If they were vandals, they'd break things, and if they were looking to steal things to resell, they'd focus on electronics, silver, jewelry, they'd access banking sites, et cetera. I'm beginning to think it's kids whose parents have either left, passed away, or are alcoholics or drug addicts, leaving the kids to fend for themselves. Do you know a family in the area whose parents have recently changed in some way? Died? Become sick?"

"Oh dear." Ms. Tisch rubbed her hands together. "This

is very disturbing." She looked at Levi and smiled. "I don't know of anyone like you describe. The only family around here that comes to mind with a sick family member is the Williams family. Mr. Williams died about two years ago, and Mrs. Williams was diagnosed just four months ago with cancer. Ovarian. She's a parishioner of my church. She has four kids between the ages of two and twelve. It's so sad. But those are good kids; they wouldn't do anything like this. I deliver meals to them once a week. And the house is maybe a bit messy, but the kids are always respectful."

She walked over to Ms. Tisch and kneeled down in front of her. "Are the kids boys or girls?"

"The baby is a girl; the others are all boys. They are eight, ten, and twelve."

She smiled into the little woman's eyes. Softly, she asked, "Did they know you'd be gone last night?"

Ms. Tisch gasped and put her hands up to her face. Her pale blue eyes watered and she slowly nodded her head.

"Thank you. We'll look further into this, but for now, we don't know anything for certain. Okay?"

Ms. Tisch took Sage's hands in hers and said, "Thank you so much."

She smiled and looked at Levi. "I'm going to head over to the office."

28

Levi smiled at Sage's retreating back; she was chomping at the bit to research the Williams family and find out all she could. He looked at Ms. Tisch and smiled, "Is there anything else you can think of that we should know?"

Ed stood staunchly by, quietly listening and writing out his report.

"I took the boys cookies last week and told Emily—Mrs. Williams—I would be gone for a few days to visit my sister."

He took her small hand in his, "We don't know for sure it's them, Ms. Tisch. But, until we do know for sure, you should stay away from them and don't let them in your house. We'll get back to you and let you know as soon as we find out who is breaking and entering." He pulled his card from his wallet and handed it to Ms. Tisch. "If you think of something, you can call me or Ed." He nodded toward Ed, leaning on a counter writing in his notebook.

"Thank you so much, Mr. Jacobson." She turned to Ed and said, "Thank you, Ed."

Levi stood and shook hands with Ed, waved to them both and left the house. He couldn't wait to get to the office and talk to Sage. She probably had it all figured out by this time; she was a whiz on the computer. He had software programs that were more in depth than most civilian access allowed, but something told him Dirks and Sam had something just that much better.

He hopped in his truck, started it, and pulled from the curb. Then, he remembered that Sage loved the chocolate sea salt caramels from Scott's Sweets and stopped in there for a morning treat.

Entering the office a few minutes later, the first thing his eyes landed on was Sage at the second desk, a laptop opened in front of her and Dirks, Sam, and Chuck leaning over her shoulders, all of them reading and whispering.

Sage looked up and beamed her brightest smile, and honest to God, his knees went weak. "I've found them, the Williamses and Carl; the boy I gave my lunch to is a Williams."

He stepped up to the desk and looked over her shoulder as much as he could. She had dossiers pulled up on the whole family. He chuckled, "What's the game plan?"

Dirks responded, "Sam and I thought we'd take Chuck over there under the guise of needing to work on the electrical service and see if we can get in and look around. Don't want to scare them if they aren't the culprits. And we'd know then if we should get a warrant and have the police search for the stolen items."

"Sounds like a great plan. Let us know what you find."

Sage's head popped up from behind her computer; she snapped, "Wait a minute, what about me?"

Levi was surprised by her tone of voice. "They've seen you, and they'll know you aren't with the electric company."

She defended, "I could be of use somewhere else, out of sight."

"Or, you can help me finish setting up for the festival. We only have a few hours left."

The men gathered their belongings, phones, coffee cups and silently left the office, sensing a fight brewing.

Sage abruptly stood and stomped over to the coffeepot, poured herself a cup and stalked back to the desk. She plopped into the chair and tapped a few more keys on the computer.

Levi poured himself some coffee and leaned against the wall across from the desk, watching her. "So, I'm getting the vibe that you're pissed."

She responded but her body and tone were of a tightly coiled wire, "This is my case. I've made contact, I've done the research, I've done everything, and you swoop in and give it to the *men* without so much as asking me if I minded or asking what I thought. My first impression was correct; you're a chauvinist."

He froze with his coffee cup halfway to his lips. "I most certainly am not. I've managed many women in my time."

"So I've heard," she snipped.

Fighting to control his temper, he responded, "Not everything you hear is true."

"Hmm."

She abruptly stood, crossed her arms over her chest and squared off with him. "What do you need me to do today?"

He glanced out the window, ground his jaw, and took a deep breath. "This is still my company, and you work for me. For the record, I don't think it was a good idea for you to go to the Williams' house, and I don't need to explain why. Today, you need to check that all of the cameras in the haunted house are working and can be accessed when needed. And if one of them isn't working, we'll go and fix it. In the meantime, I have bids to take care of and calls to make."

29

Sage seethed with anger. She methodically accessed each camera and noted which ones needed an adjustment, training the cameras on doorways and widening the view as much as she could to get the whole room. She wasn't mad; she was hurt. She let her guard down with him, and he turned around and ignored her work and effort. She absently listened as he made his phone calls to potential clients, made appointments to come out and write up bids and called to check and see if the recent installations had been satisfactory and were there any questions. Professional, knowledgeable, and friendly. She stifled the snort she wanted to let loose.

Closing the lid on her laptop, actually Dirks' laptop, she packed it up and walked toward the door. He ended his call and said, "Where are you going?"

She slowly turned to face him, "To the haunted house to adjust a couple cameras."

"I'll come with you in case you need help."

She couldn't take it. "I'm not helpless. I can do it alone, even though I'm a woman."

She pulled the door open a bit faster than she needed and quickly stepped outside, letting it close behind her. Walking briskly, she stared at the sidewalk until voices drifted up from the town square. She raised her head as the square came into view. A gathering of people filled the square with laughter and merriment. The brightly colored clothing and decorations adorned the town and mingled with the crimson leaves in the trees and those blanketing the ground. The smell of apple cider floated in the air and Sage stopped in front of the kissing booth instead of continuing to Herschfield House. The cider she'd smelled was coming from here, and two women were in the booth stirring the tasty smelling concoction and giggling. One of the women turned and saw her standing there. "Want some cider? We're trying it out before tomorrow."

"Sure, thanks."

The woman poured her a cup and handed it to her. "We were trying to decide if we should add some of the spiced booze to it or not."

Sage sipped the cider and smiled, "It's delicious as it is, but the booze would be great in it, too."

The dark-haired woman giggled and said, "You want a shot in there now?"

She chuckled, "Naw, thanks; I'm working."

"What do you do?"

Pointing toward the Hirschfield House, she said, "Security installation at the haunted house. With the recent robberies, the mayor thought it would be wise to secure it."

"Yeah, that's a bummer. We've never had anything like

that around here. You'll probably catch a lot more than theft in there tomorrow night. If you know what I mean."

A smile spread across Sage's face and she responded, "So I've heard, I guess that means it's true, and not just a rumor."

The women giggled. "Not a rumor."

The dark-haired gal asked, "Are you coming to the zombie slaying tonight?"

"Not sure; do I have to dress up?"

The blonde smiled broadly, "Only if you want to have fun. The costumes are the most fun."

They all laughed, and Sage nodded her head. "I'll see about tonight, and thanks for the cider."

She tossed her empty cup in the garbage can and continued walking toward the house. So far everyone here had been friendly and welcoming. It made her think twice about small towns, though she knew she couldn't stay. First of all, she needed work, and second of all, Levi. She couldn't lose her heart to him. Too bad, because he was something special, except for the sexist thing.

She entered the house noting the front door was open. Voices poured out from several directions, and the place had been transformed from its previous stately manor to the beginnings of a haunted house. Dark cardboard walls had been constructed and there were scary paintings of ghouls and ghosts here and there. The living room had been turned into a death chamber, with body parts strewn around and splashes of red paint to mimic blood splattered on the cardboard walls. Netting and cobwebs were hung from the ceiling with care and just low enough that it would tickle your face as you walked through it. In the daylight, it didn't look scary, but in the evening, she could see how it would transform into a haunted mansion. She waved at some of the artisans working on scaring the place up and made her way up the stairs to the back room where one of the cameras wasn't working.

It seemed as though this room would not be transformed into some ghastly laboratory of death and destruction. She moved a few cushions which had been tossed in for safekeeping and pulled a folding chair from the corner to see if she could reach the camera on the wall. She reached and stretched to no avail, cursing her short stature. She looked around for something taller to stand on and found a stool that looked like it belonged to a bar top table. It was totally out of place here, but whatever. She moved the stool to just below the camera and climbed on it, careful to keep it from swiveling and knocking her on her ass.

She slowly reached up and jiggled the wire attached to the camera. It instantly came to life, the little red light shining brightly. She reached into her back pocket and pulled out the sheet of black plastic disks to place over the light, so the public wasn't aware they were on camera. She pulled her phone from her front pocket and tapped a few times to pull up her program to test the picture. Not getting the signal she wanted she reached up again, but the stool twisted, and she had to grab the wall to keep from falling. Steadying herself again, she slowly reached up to unplug the camera, but pulling the cord from the base took more force than she thought. She lost her balance and tried grabbing the wall again.

From the corner of her eye she saw Levi run toward her, heard him yelp in pain then she lost her grip on the wall only to fall into his arms and they both tumbled to the floor. Luckily some of the cushions she'd pushed aside kept them from landing like stones. She heard him grunt and moved to roll from on top of him. He held her in place, and she turned to look into his eyes.

"Are you okay?" he huffed out.

"It appears I'm better than you. Did you hurt your leg?"

"Yeah. But, it's okay, just cramped up when I tried running toward you."

"You shouldn't have run; I was okay." She tried keeping the sarcasm at bay, but she was still hurt.

"You didn't look okay; you were falling. Off. A. Stool. That. Swivels," he clipped out.

She sat back and faced him. "The ladders were all in use. I was fine."

He sat up, grimacing a couple of times. "Sage." He let out a breath. "You can't stand on a stool when you do this work. You have to be safe."

"I was saf..." She stopped as she saw the tensing of his jaw and furrowing of his brow.

They stared into each other's eyes, and she noted that his took on a deeper tone and they were incredibly sexy. His lashes were thick and full, his skin clear, and the fullness of his lips reminded her of the many kisses they'd shared last night. He reached forward and wrapped his hand around her nape, pulled her close and kissed her on the lips. Soft kisses sent butterflies soaring in her tummy and shivers ran through her body, the dampness between her legs increased and her nipples puckered.

He pulled away just a fraction, "I'm sorry."

"For breaking my fall?" She was half joking.

He swiped his thumb across her bottom lip, the coarseness of his skin in such contrast to hers. It sent a shiver down her spine. He held her in place, his hand still on her nape, each sitting thigh to thigh, staring into each other's eyes. His voice was gruff when he softly said, "I'm sorry I didn't ask you. I just thought it would be nice to spend the day with you. Working, talking, just being."

Well, knock her over with a feather. He wanted to spend time with her? No shit. "You did?"

He huffed out a breath, "Yes. Apparently, I didn't express that correctly."

She swallowed the lump in her throat. Well, now she just felt stupid. Not having the words, she lunged at him, knocked him down, and crawled on top of him. Locking her lips onto his, she devoured his mouth; her tongue plunged in and tasted him fully. He rolled her over and covered her with his body, he ground himself into her, massaging her clit with his hardness. She whimpered and wriggled, the sweat dampening her skin, her breathing ragged. She clung to him, her hands fisting in his shirt, then sliding down and pushing his ass, urging him to move faster. He pulled away from her mouth, "Sage. There are people around the house."

"Don't care," she panted.

～

He looked up at the door, noting they were hidden behind furniture that had been pushed into this room to make way for Halloween decorations. The cushions beneath them offered some comfort. He reached between them and unzipped her jeans, then his. She quickly shimmied hers down, pulling one leg out, then quickly pushed his jeans just past his ass. She reached between them, wrapped her hand around his cock, and he groaned. She pumped him a few times then led the tip to her opening, he tightened his muscles and slid inside of her. The air left her lungs in a whoosh, and he sighed at the feel of her fisting him like a glove. Soft, warm and so damn wet, the feeling was incomparable to any pleasure he'd ever experienced. Something about the feel of her skin against his, the smell of her body and the way he fit so perfectly inside her, made him feel so differently about things.

He moved in and out of her, slowly at first, enjoying the feeling of her lips surrounding his cock. He could feel every inch as he pushed back into her silky wetness. He wanted to feel this again and again.

Looking into her eyes, he began thrusting fast and hard, and she met him move for move. She smiled at him, her full lips wet and swollen from his kisses, but so sensuous. Her small body felt perfect against his, under him. He drove deeper and moved faster, and marveled at her face tensed with the expression of beautiful ecstasy. Simply perfection. He spilled himself into her with a groan, his breath coming out in huffs.

He fell over her, holding himself up on his elbows and looked into her eyes, enjoying the darkness of color and the depth of emotion he saw in them.

She sighed and softly said, "That was fantastic."

He kissed her softly. "Yeah."

30

"I'd like to go and see the zombie paintball fight tonight; would you like to go with me?" They'd finished up the cameras, after almost getting caught in their flagrant lovemaking session, and came back to the office.

"Why?"

She glanced over at him from her desk; he was staring at his computer screen. His brows were furrowed and his sexy mouth turned down into a frown. She leaned forward on her elbows and giggled. "You're afraid you'll see Viv."

He shot her a look of disbelief and then turned back to his computer. "Don't be ridiculous."

She laughed and slapped the top of the desk. "You are too." She stood and walked to stand in front of him, her thumbs tucked into her back pockets. "She called off your date, Levi."

"It wasn't a date." He sat back in his chair and motioned her forward with his fingers. "It was a presence."

Walking to him, a sly smile on her face, she giggled. "Whatever."

When she was close enough that he could grab her, he pulled her into his lap and kissed her lips. "It wasn't a date."

The door burst open and Sam, Dirks, and Chuck walked in, stopped abruptly and stared at them. Sage jumped up, and Chuck slapped his thigh and burst out laughing. "I knew it, Sage. Remember I told you there was a reason you're here?" He walked to the counter in the back and laid the equipment he was carrying on top. "That's it. You're here to love Levi."

She jumped back like she was doused with hot water. "No one's in love here, Chuck."

"Most certainly not," Levi added. A little too quickly for Sage's comfort, which made a knot form in her stomach. She was afraid to make eye contact, so she chose to change the subject. Nodding to Dirks, she asked, "Did you get inside the Williams home?"

Dirks rubbed the top of his very short cropped hair and shook his head. "Nope. Someone was in there, but they wouldn't come to the door. We went to the church and talked to the pastor; we went to the school and talked to teachers. It appears the kids are often absent, and hungry. Homework isn't being done, and grades are falling."

Sam opened his laptop and pulled up the files he'd compiled throughout the day. Sage clicked through them, her mouth falling open. "How did you get all this data?"

He chuckled and glanced at Levi. "I have a few security clearances and the best software money can buy." She looked at him for the first time since they'd entered the office. At six foot two, he looked much larger. Broad shoulders, built arms, massive chest. The short, dark hair and deep brown eyes showed intelligence.

"Wow." She continued to look through his data. "This is simply amazing."

He half sat on the desk next to his computer, arms crossed over his chest. "You could work with this software every day if you come and work with us, Sage. You'll love it."

She stared into his eyes, then glanced at Dirks, who nodded at her and smiled. She looked at the computer again and frowned. "I really wanted to own my own security firm. It's been a lifelong dream."

"Then buy in with us." She couldn't believe this awesome opportunity was presenting itself and she had no money for it. She swallowed and glanced at Levi who sat quietly watching. She plastered on a smile, "Thanks, but I had to spend my savings on my father's medications and hospital stays." She shook her head, "I can't buy into anything right now. I'm actually here for a job."

Dirks stepped forward and turned her to face him. Hands on her shoulders, he said, "Sam and I have talked. We want you and understand your situation. We can offer you a buy-in over time. Work with us, and a portion of what you make can go to your buy-in. We'll work it out, Sage. All of it."

She stifled the sob that threatened, her hands flew to her face for just a moment, then she threw herself into Dirks' arms and hugged him tightly. "Really?"

They laughed, and in unison, said, "Really."

Dirks set her down and looked her in the eye, "Sage, I've known you for years, I know who you are. We want to work with you. You showed us what you were capable of today in locating the Williamses. Join us. Partner with us. Perhaps Levi will join us, too."

She turned to look into his eyes, hope soaring through her that this could all work out for them. "I haven't made up my mind yet, guys. It's a bit more complicated for me."

Her stomach dropped, but she tried focusing on the good thing that was happening here. She was going to own her own business; well, part of one. But with one of her best friends, so double score.

31

Shit. He'd just begun to hope she might start to love Sapphire Falls and want to stay. He'd allowed himself to think about keeping her here with him and working with her. He couldn't go back there. It would mean seeing Jenny and Tim and their kids. He'd no doubt run into them. The knot in his stomach grew and sat hard at the bottom. He wasn't going back there—ever.

"Get over it, Levi. Please." He sat at the kitchen table in his house sharing a pizza with Sam. "Have you ever thought that seeing them again might finally release you from the hatred and heartache you've hung on to all these years?"

He slammed back his beer and jumped up to toss the bottle. "Levi, please consider it. They live over in Cumberland County now; you probably won't ever see them. Don't let her ruin something great—again. You've let her control your whole fucking life."

He leaned on the counter, his palms flat on the top, and hung his head down. Closing his eyes, he tried to picture her, but he'd lost the image years ago. He barely remembered a good time with her, happy days, or even being in love. What kind of dumbass was he to let someone who didn't deserve him in the first place dictate his whole life? Stupid.

"I don't know, Sam. I need to think about it some more."

"Fair enough. How about Sage? Would you come for her if she asked?"

Turning to look his friend in the eye, he shook his head, "She won't ask. It's not like that."

Laughing, Sam responded, "Not like what? You're screwing her; you clearly enjoy spending time with her. You stare at her all the time. It's why you didn't want to go out with the redhead, isn't it?"

"She's too flashy."

Sam laughed. Standing, he grabbed the empty pizza box and tossed it into the wastebasket. "And Sage isn't. She's bright, funny, independent, and strong. She's positively perfect for you." Sam slapped him on the back and walked to his bedroom, whistling a happy tune.

Glancing at the clock on the wall, he grabbed his cell phone from the counter, turned the dishwasher on, and left the house to play paintball and zombies against zombie slayers. Not something he was interested in doing, so he thought he'd let himself get shot and sit somewhere with some booze and tie one on.

He pulled up to the Rise & Shine and glanced over at the town square. You could see it from here if you looked between the grocery store and the diner. People were gathering about, excited for the festival kickoff tomorrow. As some of the carnival people came into town, it brought out the locals too excited to wait. They'd go down to the square, watch the setup and maybe meet someone new.

He stepped out of his truck, walked up the front steps of the bed and breakfast and walked in the front door. A few guests sat in the living room chatting; he absently waved at them and ascended the steps to Sage's room. She was in there; the door was open, and he could hear her talking. He silently pushed the door open just a crack and there lay Dirks across the bed, head resting on his hand, leaning on his elbow. His stomach roiled and bile formed. He looked up from Dirks and Sage was on the settee in the corner of the room, lacing up her boots. She wore camo pants, her marching boots, an Army green long-sleeve t-shirt and her hair was pulled back into a ponytail, creating a chocolate brown trail over her shoulder as she bent.

Her eyes landed on his, the smile bright and friendly. "Hi, come on in. We're just working out some details of the business."

Dirks sat up and nodded, "Levi." He stood and nodded. "We just need one more piece to finish our puzzle. Sure wish you'd join us."

His jaw ticked as his teeth mashed together. His worst fear reared its ugly head, finding the woman he lov... Walking in on something that would crash his world one more time. His eyes darted between Sage and Dirks; his spine stiffened, and he had trouble breathing. "I'm thinking about it, Dirks."

Sage stood, hands on her hips. "Are you going to go like that? You'll get paint all over your good clothes."

"We'll see. I'll wait for you downstairs." He turned and descended the steps; his footfalls harder than necessary. He felt like a robot, stiff and unyielding. Reaching the front door, he bounded down the steps, his stride wider than it needed to be seeking his truck and safety.

Climbing into the driver's side he put his hands on the wheel and took deep breaths. The passenger door opened, and Sage slid into the truck without a word.

She turned toward him, her hand rested softly on his shoulder. "Hey, we're just friends. He's like my brother and nothing more. We've spent years together in war and out and we're comfortable with each other. What you saw was my friend, Dirks, telling me about the business and the things we still need to work out and how I fit in and all about Bourbonville, Kentucky."

He swallowed and turned to gaze into her eyes. Sincerity showed in the glassy brown depths, her full dark lashes the perfect frame. Her face was petite and perfectly shaped and the most appealing face he'd ever laid eyes on.

He nodded slightly, "I know." His voice was soft and raspy. "It just hit me wrong, I guess. I wasn't expecting it." He swallowed the lump that had formed in his throat. His hand slowly cupped her jaw as he stared into her eyes.

A slow smile graced her lips, and her fingers brushed his face, smoothing away the lines. It was as if her touch could heal; she seemed to wipe away all worry as she touched him. Her light strokes and soft breathing a salve for a wound. "I understand. I'm not her." She held his face firm as he tried to turn away from her. "I'm me. I'm loyal, above all else."

His eyes stung as tears threatened and he swallowed furiously to keep his emotions in check. His voice sounded foreign to him when he heard it. "Sage. I can't…"

Her lips softly touched his, almost pleading for him to feel her. Her tongue lightly licked across his bottom lip, nipping delicately, then she kissed where she nipped.

"Fight it, Levi. Beat those bad memories and visions away with me. Let's start over, you and me."

He rested his forehead against hers, willing his breathing to return to normal. Sweat trickled down his back, her scent, the fresh, clean aroma of a spring morning and the wash hanging on the line, swirled around them and his eyes closed as he allowed her to seep into him from every sense. Her soft breathing soothed him; her gentle touch pulled the negative from him, and he simply let go.

They sat that way until his back screamed for him to straighten up. He touched his lips to hers and sat back, stretching lightly. Lost for words, he started the truck and she giggled. "Now, let's go kill some zombies."

He chuckled and pulled away from the curb.

32

The drive to Travis Bennett's farm was scenic and peaceful. Did she and Levi just move in a direction that melded them together? Her heart hammered in her chest, and her hands shook. This was new territory for her; she didn't know how to process these new feelings. And then she thought about moving away and living somewhere else. He didn't seem interested in moving back to his home state, even though she'd be there—because of his ex. The ex kept winning. It was hard to compete with someone you'd never met; beating the unknown was always like running a marathon and not knowing where the finish line was.

He turned down a road, and the fields striped with rows of cut cornstalks sped by the windows. The scenery soon turned to trees and then the little white house appeared in front of a field of standing hay. He parked along the drive behind the other vehicles, and she jumped out of the truck thinking running through the fields with a paintball gun in her hand would help her process all of these emotions. He caught up to her, took her hand in his and said close to her ear, "Thank you for talking me down. Or up. Or whatever, but thank you."

She glanced up into his handsome face and smiled. "You're welcome."

He squeezed her hand and shivers ran down her spine. A cool breeze blew over them, and she found herself grateful for it to ease the heat crawling through her body. Alongside the house was a rack set up with paintball guns and paintballs. Groups of people were gathered around loading their weapons and chattering animatedly about the games and the rules. You had to choose whether to be a slayer or a zombie. Slayers had bright pink paintballs, zombies bright green. No question for Sage, slayer all the way.

Levi walked over to the guns, picked one up and headed to the green paintballs. Okay, opposite sides. She'd make sure to shoot him first. They were each handed a white t-shirt, slayer written across hers, zombie across his. She smiled at him, tapped him on the shoulder and said, "See you in the dead zone, zombie."

She quickly walked to the side of the field where the slayers were preparing to shoot their prey. She loaded her gun and watched Levi walk to the opposite side. Then she recognized the red hair and heard the vibrant laugh of Viv, who was also on the zombie side of the field and her heart hammered in her chest. They were on the same side. Viv reached up and touched his arm, and he smiled down into her face. Viv lived here, and so did Levi. They'd probably eventually end up together anyway, hopefully after she was gone, but it tore a hole in her stomach, and she felt queasy and unsteady. It might just be better if she left right after the festival ended tomorrow night. She could get to Dirks' place in twelve hours or so and take a nap once she arrived. Leaving at midnight, she'd be there in time for lunch.

A clean break would be better than drawing this out and falling in love with him. She watched him talking to Viv, the bright smile on Viv's face as she looked into his. Tears stung her eyes as she thought about all that could be, but wouldn't because he couldn't get past his ex. She backed up slowly, fading into the darkness around her. She turned the corner to the opposite side of the house, leaned her gun against the wall where it would be found along with her shirt and began her long walk home. She'd marched countless miles in the Army; this would be a breeze and give her the time it took her to settle down so sleep would claim her as soon as she hit the bed.

33

"Levi?" He turned and saw Viv bounding toward him, her zombie shirt with its florescent paint seemed boring and sedate against her effervescent personality. Her hair again looked like a bright red bird's nest; dangly sparkly earrings twinkled in the dim lights from the deck.

He took a deep breath, "Hey, Viv; how are you?"

"I'm great. As soon as I shoot him, I'd like to introduce you to my new man." She laughed and then corrected herself, "I mean with a paintball gun." She held up her weapon. "I've known him for some time. He's a truck driver who comes into the diner all the time. He asked me out, and as soon as he did, I realized he was the man under my nose all the time. I hope you didn't mind that I canceled our date." She laid her hand on his upper arm and squeezed.

"Viv, I was disappointed, but I'm very happy you found someone. So the gypsy's magic wove itself around you, I see."

The redhead giggled, "It sure did." He turned his head to look for Sage and couldn't see her anywhere. She was so small that she could slip in between people and not be noticed. It was probably what made her good at surveillance. As beautiful as she was, she could also be a bit of a chameleon. Viv chattered on and on, and he strained to find the woman he wanted to see more than anything else in the world.

The air horn blew, and the game was on. He ran and took cover behind a grouping of trees, firing only when necessary to keep his location secret. He silently moved to a large bush and then slowly made his way toward the river; that's where she'd go. He saw how she stared at the river when they'd investigated the cottage a few days ago. Careful to avoid potholes and divots in the terrain, he stood still to listen for footsteps and shooting. His eyes adjusted to the dim light. The moon's illumination only about one percent, gave him the cover he needed to continue to the water's edge.

He heard harsh breathing and slowed his progress, kneeling down to hide himself. The sounds to his left became more pronounced, and he realized it was two people having sex. He smirked and slowly advanced his position.

The edge of Travis' property was high above the water, and he sat down to massage the ache in his leg. Watching the dim light of the moon reflect on the ripples in the water relaxed him. His thoughts turned to Sage and his life as it was now. It was richer and more vibrant with her in it. He looked forward to seeing her every day. He loved watching her work on a project, the concentration on her face, her excitement when finding a nugget of information, and the efficiency she used to attack every asset of any assignment. But on the personal front, he loved talking to her, enjoying her presence, even just riding in the truck not saying anything. The aroma of her perfume, the sound of her voice, the cadence of her laugh, it all spoke to him on a level so far above any he'd ever been on.

Was it enough to overcome the fear of seeing Jenny and her family? More to the point, finally facing his former best friend Tim, would be harder than seeing her. The betrayal from someone you trusted with your future wife, with your secrets, with your family. Tim and Sam and Levi grew up together, went to school together and had been friends until the betrayal came to light. Then both he and Sam had left Tim in the past. He'd gone off to the Army thinking he was leaving for a short time and would return to marry Jenny; instead, he never went back there to live. He'd buried his parents and returned to whatever base he was stationed at without ever seeing anyone he knew outside of the family.

Pulling his phone from his back pocket, he checked the time. Nine-thirty. He decided to make his away across the ridge and see if he could find Sage. He tripped over some brush, swore silently, then righted himself and continued. Feeling his phone vibrate, he pulled it from his pocket to see a text from Sage. "*Not feeling well, walked home. Have fun.*"

His brow furrowed. Walked home? It was probably three, no, four miles from here. He quickly typed out, "*Are you okay?*"

He waited for a few minutes, turning toward his truck just down the drive when his phone vibrated in his hand. "*Fine. Just need some rest.*"

Not sure if she needed someone to help her or just leave her be, he decided to go home. Tomorrow would be enough of a trying day for them at the office with the festival in full swing.

34

S age softly climbed the stairs—weary, sad, and oddly lonely. Feeling like a wounded animal, she silently unlocked the door to her room and slipped inside. Removing her boots, she slumped back into the cream colored settee and stared at the ceiling. "Shit," she said to no one.

Standing, she stretched, pulled her duffel bag from the closet and began packing her clothes. Having to rearrange her clothing from the usual way she packed to accommodate the new clothes she'd purchased to impress a man who clearly wasn't interested in impressing her. She undressed to pack the clothes on her back, leaving only the clothes she'd wear tomorrow on the bed. She slipped between the sheets, inhaled the fresh aroma of the bedding and mentally checked purchasing laundry soap on her way to Dirks'.

After a fitful night, Sage awoke, her eyes puffy and every muscle screaming at her for not taking a warm bath to loosen her tense muscles. She turned the water on in the shower to the hottest temperature she thought she could endure and stood under the stream willing herself to relax. This was going to be a hard damn day. Emotionally, not physically.

She quickly dressed and tiptoed downstairs to check out and grab some coffee. She loaded her gear into her car and ate breakfast in the dining room with the other guests, all excitedly regaling each other with their zombie killing expertise. She only half listened, her mind on the easiest way to avoid Levi today and slipping out of town later. Dirks lightly punched her on the shoulder and sat next to her at the table. "Penny for your thoughts."

She giggled, "Bargain basement there, Dirks. These thoughts are worth at least ten bucks."

"That right? Clue me in." He shoveled loads of scrambled eggs into his mouth, and she shook her head. The man could eat. Between him and Chuck, she'd seen more food consumed this week than she'd seen in any Army mess hall.

"So, I'm heading to Kentucky tonight. Still hide the key to your place in the flower pot on the front porch?"

He stopped shoveling and stared at her while he chewed. He nodded. His brows furrowed and around the pile of eggs in his mouth, he said, "What's up?"

She faked a smile, "Nothing. I'm excited to get to work; that's all. I figure if I get there a day or two before you, I can look for an apartment and settle in somewhere so when you and Sam get there, I'll be ready to dive in."

He nodded, swallowed and responded. "You can stay

with me as long as you want. I have three bedrooms, and only one is being used. Plus, it'll save you some money so you can catch up. Don't rush, 'k?"

She nodded and sipped her coffee, food unappealing this morning.

"Everything okay with you and Levi?"

"Sure," she responded quickly, swallowing the sob that threatened to strangle her.

She glanced around at the other guests and felt a bit jealous of their carefree chatter. The world was on her shoulders this morning and she was struggling under the weight of it.

"I'll see you at the office, okay? I'm going to take a bit of a walk before work." She playfully shoved him as he continued to inhale the food in front of him. She rolled her eyes at one of the women at the table who watched Dirks with a hint of disgust on her face.

Sage walked toward the square, particularly drawn to the gypsy, Liz's trailer. She slowly skirted the area around it, the brightly colored hanging lanterns swaying in the breeze. The sun was just rising above the sky, and the fresh coating of leaves on the ground blanketed the area in a mesmerizing display of color and vibrancy. Sitting on a bench close to Liz's Vardo, she silently prayed for guidance and strength. As if appearing from nowhere, Liz stood next to the bench, startling Sage, her heart racing.

Liz smiled down at her and pointed to the empty seat next to her. Today she wore brightly colored clothing, a flowing silky skirt in reds and purples, scarves in a myriad of colors hanging from the waist and gently kissing the leaves on the ground.

Sage scooted over and patted the bench. "You should be in security; you're quiet as a ghost."

Liz laughed, a gentle lilt to her voice. "I've been called many things. I don't believe ghost is one of them." Liz gently rubbed stones in her hands and turned to face Sage. "I sense that you are heavyhearted this morning. Do you need to talk?"

Sage smiled, "I'm not much of a bare-my-heart kind of girl." She rubbed her hands together and stared down at her newly-purchased brown boots with the cute buckles.

"Ah, well, it's good then that I can feel what's wrong without words." She gently took Sage's hands and placed the stones she'd been rubbing into them. Closing her fingers around the stones, Liz looked deep into her eyes. "The stones carry healing powers and positive vibrations."

Sage was mesmerized by the brown eyes looking into her soul. "You worry about your choices and if you are making good ones." Liz moved the hair that had slid over Sage's shoulders. "A fresh start is waiting for you and the promise of all new and exciting things is your reward. You have good vibrations coming from you, Sage."

Liz smiled a knowing smile; her eyes seemed to gleam in the dim morning light. She emanated a brightness. She stood and walked slowly toward the door to her Vardo, without another word. Sage watched her disappear inside and looked at the stones in her hands. Smooth glassy stones reflected a myriad of colors, and weirdly, Sage felt emboldened to begin her new life.

35

Pacing the office early in the morning, Levi worried about the task ahead. They thought they knew who the thieves were, but they weren't positive, and frankly, it was dangerous to assume and let someone else slip through the cracks. The majority of the townspeople would be at the festival tonight, meaning their homes would be empty. How in the hell were they supposed to keep track of a whole town, the haunted house, and the festival?

Then, there was Sage. She would be leaving soon, and he hated to think of the day. After this festival was over, as soon as tomorrow, he'd ask her out on a proper date, so they could sit and talk, eat and enjoy each other. He wanted to know what she thought about things. Everything. And he needed that time with her to decide whether or not to go home. It would be impossible to go home to Bourbonville and work with Sage every day and not be with her. In every sense. And the thought of her dating someone else tore at his heart more than thinking about Jenny and Tim.

He stopped pacing. That was a revelation. He rubbed his nape, closed his eyes and tried once again to conjure up the image of Tim and Jenny together. Nothing.

He poured himself a cup of coffee and instantly the color reminded him of Sage—her deep brown eyes, always sparkling when she talked. He loved seeing the excitement on her face when she was onto something and the easy manner in which she dealt with Dirks, Sam, and Chuck. She would do well with those guys in the business.

The door swung open, and Chuck entered the office carrying bags of food. "Hey, Boss. I figured we'd be working hard today, so I brought donuts, sweets from Scott's, and some candy bars to stuff in our pockets."

He grinned. "That's thoughtful of you, Chuck. Thanks."

Chuck ambled his large frame around the office as he laid the food out on the back counter. He poured himself a cup of coffee, went for a donut, and promptly shoved it into his mouth. With his mouth full, he said, "Have one, Boss; they're fresh."

Stepping back to the counter, Levi grabbed a cream cheese Danish and sat at his desk. "Okay, Chuck, do you know where you're at today?"

"Yep. I'm going to be circling the square, watching for anything amiss."

He nodded. Sam and Dirks came in, and Dirks headed straight to the display of donuts. "Awesome." He grabbed two donuts and plopped his laptop on top of the second desk.

Sam sat at the desk, opened his computer, and began typing. "I've got this grid mapped out like you asked, Levi. Sage can stay here in the office, monitoring the haunted house. We can stay in touch with each other via our phones and headsets in the field. Dirks is going to monitor the Williams' house and the kids. He'll be in this area here." He turned his computer toward Levi and the others leaned over to see the grid.

"I'll be on the north and east side of town, canvassing the areas for anything suspicious. You'll be on the west and south side of town. It should work. All we really need to do is make sure no burglaries happen, and hopefully, catch the little shits doing it. Thoughts?"

"Many, but that looks great."

The door opened, and Sage entered, looking tired but fabulous. The orange sweater she wore hugged her slight curves. The jeans and boots showcased her lithe legs. She wore her long dark hair down, quickly becoming his favorite style. The soft locks flowed around her shoulders and gleamed. However, the smile she wore seemed forced. Her voice was soft when she spoke, "Morning, guys."

Chuck held up his donut, "I brought sweets to get us rolling this morning."

She smiled, grabbed a cup of coffee and walked over to survey the pile of food. "Wow, you're going to be climbing the walls."

Sam turned his computer toward Sage. "Here's the game plan today, girl. You ready?"

She leaned over the desk and read the grid and plan. She stood and nodded, "Let's do this."

Dirks set his laptop on the second desk as Sage sat at the chair. She queued up the software for the cameras at the haunted house. She'd barely given him a glance when she came into the office. His stomach churned.

The group chatted, ate and shot the breeze until it was time to head to their positions. They grabbed their jackets, Levi waiting until he was alone with Sage. He walked behind the desk, turned her chair to face him and leaned down to eye level with her. "What's going on?"

She sat a bit straighter. "Weren't you listening? We have a festival going on today. You have the west and south side of town; I've got the haunted house. You really need to pay attention, Levi."

He took a deep breath, "What's going on with you. And me. You've barely looked at me this morning. And, how are you today? Still sick?" He looked into her eyes, clear and beautiful as always.

"No, must have been something I ate yesterday. I'm good today." She looked past him at nothing in particular and the sinking feeling that had begun to settle in his stomach solidified itself.

"Sage. Do we need to talk about anything?"

She rolled her shoulders, took a deep breath and looked into his eyes. "No. It's all good."

He stood abruptly, irritated that she couldn't or wouldn't talk to him and stalked to the coatrack, grabbed his jacket, and exited the office.

36

S age's shoulders sank. The look on Levi's face made her stomach churn, and a headache had already formed at the base of her skull. She should have just bucked up and said she was leaving tonight, but she didn't think she could do that without crying. She was on the verge of it now; falling for him hard and fast came out of nowhere. It'd been the last thing on her mind when she came here, and certainly when she'd first met him, she'd thought anything but. But now, her heart was breaking to be leaving him behind. He was the first man she'd felt a kinship with.

She glanced over the cameras in the haunted house, noting just a few workers putting up the last-minute decorations. The kitchen had been transformed into a spooky laboratory, complete with Jell-O brains, blood dripping from a bowl of rolled lasagna noodles to simulate intestines, and a dead body without a head on the counter with blood dripping from the neck. It was looking spooky indeed.

She grabbed another cup of coffee and listened to the

guys talk on their headsets, announcing that they'd arrived at their destinations. When she heard Levi's silky voice float over her speakers, her heart sped up, and her stomach threatened to relieve itself of breakfast. His sad eyes and worried brow filled the visions in her mind.

To take her mind from her sorrow, she filtered through the cameras at the haunted house again, room by room. She froze as she came to the room she and Levi had made love in, her neck stiffening up, further increasing the throbbing at the base of her skull. Besides the memory of them there, Carl—the boy she'd given her lunch to, now known as Carl Williams—was there looking through the cushions and absently stored objects in the room. He appeared to be looking for something specific.

She turned on her headset, placed it around her head and calmly announced, "Guys, Carl Williams is in the haunted house, rifling through the spare room upstairs where the furniture and paintings are stored."

Levi's voice was first to respond, "I'm not far from there. Chuck, where are you?"

"At the gazebo, but I can be to the house in a minute."

"Stay outside in case he gets spooked and makes a run for it. Watch the area for his brothers."

Sam chimed in, "I'm not far from there. I'll take up watch on the north side of the house. Do you still have eyes on him, Sage?"

"Affirmative. He appears to be looking for something. He's moved the cushions from the sofas and looked behind objects; now he's opening the closet door."

She could hear Levi running, his heavy breathing sounding through his headset and her first thought was that his leg would cramp. Fisting and releasing her fingers, she tried to breathe slowly and evenly while keeping an eye on Carl.

Levi breathlessly spoke into his headset, "I'm here and going in. I won't talk much once inside so he can't hear. Where are you Mac and Chuck?"

"Mac here, on the north side of the building. No sign of the brothers."

"Chuck here, out back, southeast corner. No brothers."

Sage scanned the cameras for Levi's presence and saw him moving up the stairs. She glanced at the camera that showed Carl, still unaware of anyone moving toward him. She softly told the guys of his actions.

Levi waved two fingers from his forehead in a makeshift salute as he slowly passed a camera in the upstairs hallway. Butterflies took flight in her tummy at the sight of his handsome face, and the deliberation he demonstrated as he approached his target. It was exciting watching him in action; his expertise was evident in his posture, carefulness, and concentration. Sexy.

Her heart rate increased, and her palms grew damp. She alternated between watching Levi hunt and Carl rummage. Carl suddenly stopped and turned his head toward the doorway.

"Levi, he may have heard you," she whispered into the microphone.

She checked the hall camera and watched Levi freeze. He glanced both directions, shot a glance at the camera and then pointed toward the door to the storage room.

Watching Carl, Sage softly said, "He's stepping toward the door, Levi." Carl moved as if he knew someone was watching, glancing side to side, then she watched as he spotted a dresser next to the doorway. He approached the dresser and opened the top drawer, lifting the linens neatly folded and resting inside.

"He's rummaging through a dresser next to the door. Be careful that he can't see you if he glances out."

Carl methodically opened drawer after drawer, until he reached the bottom drawer.

"He's in the bottom drawer now."

Carl pulled a blanket from the bottom drawer and a silk nightgown. He held the silky material up high in front of himself and glanced closely at the neckline. Seemingly satisfied with his find, he turned to the blanket and checked the silk band around the edge. Finding some embroidery on one of the corners, he lightly ran his fingers over the fine threads and bunched it and the gown together and moved toward the door.

"Levi, he's leaving the room."

She watched as Levi ducked into the next room, and Carl walked past him down the hall.

Whispering, Levi said, "I'll follow him out; we can't do anything until he leaves the building to show intent to steal. He's heading toward the back door. Chuck, get ready."

Waiting for Carl to clear the hallway and round the corner, Levi softly stepped into the hall and followed Carl down the stairs. The back stairway was closed off to the public, so it was empty of people and decorations. As soon as Carl opened the back door, Levi said, "He's out. Don't lose him."

At that point, Sage had no eyes on the men or Carl. She listened intently and could hear the rustling of leaves and Chuck's labored breathing as he said, "Gotcha." And then there was a tussle. She heard Levi approach them, and heard him howl as something happened to him. Chuck breathlessly asked, "Levi, you all right?"

Levi grunted, "Fine."

Sam came over the headset. "Got 'im, Sage, call the police."

"Roger." She picked up her phone and called Ed.

The rest of the afternoon was rather uneventful. The men spoke very little, each watching their grid and Sage continued watching the haunted house, getting a chuckle here and there as some of the patrons screamed their way through the ghoulish rooms. Men made their moves on the women, and some of the workers enjoyed themselves immensely as they found their creations working.

Levi's headset went silent as he joined Ed at the police station. She wondered for the hundredth time how he was and what was wrong with him. The guys had assured her that he'd just cramped up and then Carl had kicked him good and hard in his bad leg but that nothing was broken.

Glancing at the clock, and seeing that she only had an hour left before she left Sapphire Falls for good, tears sprang to her eyes. She sniffed and wiped her nose when Dirks teased, "You eating something spicy, Sage?"

"No," she managed.

"Sounds like it. Nose running, sniffing. Either that or you're crying. That it?"

She closed her eyes. "No."

"Hmm. Maybe you don't want to leave tonight."

"What? Sage, you're leaving tonight?" Chuck genuinely sounded disappointed.

She swallowed. "Yeah. I need to get settled in in Bourbonville before I start working in a couple of days, so I'm heading out tonight."

"Levi didn't say anything about it today. We could have

said a proper goodbye. Will you be there when we're finished for the night?"

She held her hand over the microphone and took a deep breath letting it out slowly, "I don't think so, Chuck. I just want to make this painless. Okay? You're doing great, by the way. Levi is lucky to have you."

"You too, Sage. You're going to be awesome in your new job. I honestly wish I were going with you."

Dirks came on, "Come with us, Chuck. We could use you. We just got another big job today at a horse ranch in Lexington and we'll need the help."

It was silent for a moment before Chuck responded, "It wouldn't be fair to leave Levi; he gave me a chance when no one else would. But the offer makes me happy. Maybe someday."

The men bantered back and forth, and Sage sat back in her chair, chuckling as they teased and cajoled each other. It felt just like old times in the barracks.

37

Levi's bones hurt. He'd been kicked so damn hard it rattled his teeth. He wrestled with Carl as Chuck tried holding him, and for a twelve-year-old, he was a scrappy little shit. He'd been knocked on his ass, and right now, a warm bath and Sage in his arms was the only thing that sounded like a healing balm. Then, he'd get to the bottom of what was bothering her.

Closing the door on his truck and wearily walking into the office, his eyes landed on Sage leaning on the front of her desk, her knuckles white as she gripped the edge of the desk tightly. His jaw immediately clenched. "Hi."

She took a deep breath, "Hi. Are you okay?"

"Will be. Right now I'm sore and exhausted. I'm too old to wrestle with a twelve-year-old."

He watched her face, and his stomach clenched. Normally the sparkle in her eyes shone bright; tonight it was more than just being tired. She was tense, and her posture was rigid, trying to act nonchalant.

"What's the story with Carl?"

He pulled his jacket off and hung it on a hook. Wearily

he turned, "Mom's dying...soon. The boys have been stealing food to eat. Mom doesn't have insurance. She's held housekeeping jobs here and there over time, but nothing since about a year ago. The insurance money they got from his dad's death is long gone. They stole diapers for their baby sister, clothing for Mom because she's cold all the time. The three boys found a shopping cart and stole the water heater because theirs wasn't working. The computer games they played was because the kids don't have anything at home but work and worry."

"God, that's so sad. Why the nightgown and blanket from the Hirschfield House?"

"Mom worked for them years ago. She'd embroidered on the nightgown and blanket and was telling the boys the story about it and how it was the prettiest work she'd ever done. Carl wanted her to see it again before she died."

A tear trickled down Sage's cheek, and she quickly swiped it away. She swallowed and took a deep breath. "I'm leaving. Tonight."

Gutshot. That's how he felt. He tried willing himself to move, but he couldn't. Searching her eyes for a sign that she was joking, he saw only sadness.

"I don't understand." He swallowed. "What happened last night, Sage?"

She stood and paced to the back counter, turned and walked to the desk, then back again. "I saw you and Viv talking, and it hit me that you both live here, I don't. You could have someone here who cares for you and I'll be gone soon anyway." Her voice broke, and she wiped her face with shaking fingers. "I may as well rip the bandage off and move on. You don't seem interested in joining us in Kentucky, so, I guess, that's a sign...that..." A sob ripped from her throat, and he stepped forward to touch her, but she held her hand up to halt him. His gut twisted, and his heart hammered so rapidly he felt dizzy.

"Sage. I didn't say I wouldn't go; I want to think about it." His voice cracked.

Taking a deep breath, she rubbed her hands together in front of her, "It's better this way, isn't it?"

"No, it isn't."

"Levi, I can't not fall in—"

Dirks, Sam, and Chuck walked into the office, "Hey, great job today everyone; that was awesome." Sam's friendly happy voice split the tension in the room.

"How're you doing, Levi? That kid kicked you pretty hard." Chuck quickly walked to the back of the room and looked through the leftover donuts, found one, and took a big bite.

Finding his voice, Levi responded, "I'm fine, Chuck, a bit sore, but fine."

Dirks walked to Sage and lightly punched her shoulder, "Great job today on the camera and surveillance, Sage."

Her lips hitched up on one side, and she tucked her silky strands behind her ear. "Thanks. It was fun." She clapped her hands together once and said, "I'll be hitting the road now. Chuck, great job, again." She turned to Dirks and Sam, "See you guys in Kentucky." She halted when she looked into Levi's eyes and he willed her to say she'd changed her mind. But her soft, sweet voice belied the pain her eyes held. "Good luck, Levi."

She strode out the door of the office, and he had to sit down to keep from falling.

38

S age jogged through the town square, easily skirting the late-night partiers and made it to her car in a matter of a few minutes. Opening the door and quickly starting it, she pulled from the curb in front of the bed and breakfast and easily made it through the dark, mostly-empty streets and then onto the highway. It was better this way. She'd lost so much in the past year— her money, her father, her place to live. Well, that was her choice, leaving her sad, gray hometown. But, losing Levi; this one hurt deep in her heart. A sob tore through her, and she burst into tears. Blinking furiously to see the road through the watery haze, she turned the radio up and tried to focus on the music and the highway and not her broken heart.

∼

B leary-eyed and weary to the bone, Sage located Dirks' little house on the outskirts of Bourbonville, Kentucky. The landscape had turned a few hours ago, the bright fall colors changing to the greenest grasses she'd ever seen, the lush flowers still shining brightly in the warm, humid climate. She'd opened her car windows as the sun came up and let the fresh air blow through her car and her very being. "Out with the old life, in with the new." She'd bellowed out over her radio. Liz had said as much; she had a new life waiting for her, and she was looking forward to this new life.

She found the key and let herself into Dirks' house. It was light and airy; the kitchen was painted bright yellow and little white lace curtains framed the window above the sink. An oak table pushed to the wall held a little pot of brightly colored flowers in shades of orange, yellow, and red. Sage chuckled. Who knew Dirks had such a decorative touch? She wandered into the living room and saw a beautiful leather sectional facing a large sixty-inch flat screen on the wall, an oak stand below it holding a myriad of video games, DVDs, and a stereo system to rival a local radio station. Continuing to the hall just out of the living room, it split and went in opposite directions. One bedroom and a bathroom on one end, two bedrooms on the other.

The larger of the two looked to be the master, and that had its own bathroom. Dirks had pictures on his wall of himself and friends from different duty stations all over the world. She'd found herself in several of the photos. All of them were happy pictures and showed the plethora of friends they'd each gathered through their time in active duty. Smiling, she turned and walked to the bedroom at the other end of the short hallway and dropped her duffel bag on the floor. Using the bathroom just outside the door of her new bedroom, she quickly washed up and made her way to the bed calling her name. Flopping on the bed, she stared at the ceiling for a matter of three seconds before sleep claimed her.

~

The following morning, Levi watched Sam from his window, as he climbed into his rented truck and drove away. He turned in his empty kitchen, which he'd found peaceful and relaxing just two weeks ago, but now it was lifeless and unhappy. It held no fond memories, no true signs a life lived here. He'd never hung anything on the walls, never actually made it a home, eating out most meals and coming home only to sleep. What kind of life had he actually made here?

He'd slept like shit last night, and Sam was right—that bastard; he was letting Jenny and Tim dictate his life. That was no way to live. And, it had honestly been so many years that he had no feeling anymore on those two, just the anger that he'd hung onto to keep from feeling. He was pathetic.

Taking a deep breath, he headed to the bedroom to get ready for work. He'd check his new clients as he did each morning, do some of the dreaded paperwork, figure out his day and Chuck's and keep on keeping on. But, something had to change for him. He had to start living.

39

Driving into town, he smiled to himself as some of the familiar surroundings barraged his mind. The sultry air permeated the cab of his truck and rifled through his hair from the window he'd opened. He waved at the older gentleman crossing the intersection in front of the general store, the old man absently waving back as he shuffled his feet along. The brick buildings were neatly kept, flower boxes hung from most of the storefront windows, bourbon barrels cut in half every few feet proudly held large colorful blooms of varying colors. As he drove Main Street, he smiled as he passed the bank. The hardware store boldly announced a fall sale. The little hair salon displayed a neon mirror on the side of the building, and a smaller sign below said walk-ins welcome.

His GPS announced, "You have reached your destination." In the robotic voice, he'd always thought he'd like to replace—Darth Vader or General Patton's voices would be fun for a change. He found the sign he was looking for, pulled to the curb in front and took a deep breath as he got out of his truck. He stretched and rubbed his ass; he'd been sitting for hours.

He walked into the offices of Bluegrass Security Company and froze. Sage sat behind a big desk, dwarfing her tiny body. Her dark hair was pulled into a high ponytail, the dark silky strands resting over her shoulder. She typed furiously into her computer. A soft smile on her face made his heart race. She finally glanced at him, and her fingers froze.

"Morning, Sunshine."

She swallowed and slowly stood.

"You start work early. Are they working you to death?"

She slowly shook her head, "I don't sleep much these days, so I give up and come into the office."

He stepped forward until he was standing alongside her desk. Her eyes sought his, her soft lips quivered. Reaching forward, he cupped her jaw with shaking fingers, his thumb lightly caressing her cheek. "I missed you, Sage."

She sobbed, and her hand rushed up to cover her mouth, her eyes teared, and a glistening trail slid down her soft skin.

She finally removed her hand and whispered, "Levi."

He dipped down and kissed her soft lips, warm and pliable. His tongue sought hers, dancing and dueling as his heart beat out a rapid rhythm in his chest. He pulled her into his arms and squeezed her to him, needing the feel of her body close to his.

She pulled away. "Why are you here?"

He chuckled, "I was hoping you had a job opening."

She pushed away from him and cautiously said, "Don't tease me. Why are you here?"

Shoving his thumbs into his pockets, he responded,

"I'm your new partner, Sunshine. Sam and I have been working out the details. I've been wrapping up my business in Sapphire Falls these past few weeks."

Her eyes grew large, as a smile teased her lips. "For real?"

"For real."

She sucked in a deep breath and lunged into his arms. Her arms wrapped around his shoulders and hung on tightly. Her voice was muffled by her arms and tears, "Took you long enough."

He laughed. "Impatient?"

"Lonely."

He kissed her fully and set her on her feet; he stepped back to look into her eyes, "I love you, Sage. I didn't realize it until you were gone. I love you."

Tears rained down, and she swiped furiously at them, losing the battle. "I love you, too. It broke my heart to leave, but I didn't think you cared, and I thought it would be better if I were out of the way."

Removing the tears on her face with his thumbs, he squatted to eye level, "Moving forward, I'd appreciate it if you let me decide what's good for me and I'll try and do a better job of communicating with you. Deal?"

She wrapped her arms around his shoulders and squeezed, "Deal."

Continue reading for a sneak peek at **Finish Line**, the next Bluegrass Security novel.

SNEAK PEEK

The End of **Heart Thief, Bluegrass Security Book One.**

Get book #2 of the Bluegrass Security series, Finish Line, now.

Continue reading for a Sneak Peek at Finish Line, the next novel in the Bluegrass Security Series.

CHAPTER 1 OF FINISH LINE

Stevie Jorgenson leaned against the bar stool, hiking her heel up behind her to hang on the metal rung. She'd been here at the Brass Rail Saloon, for the better part of an hour—it was her relaxation. She came in after her day was done, had a couple of bourbons, beat a few guys at pool and strutted home—hopefully with a few extra dollars in her pocket. She preferred playing for a buck and a drink, which usually meant she drank for free and made a little money.

Picking up the drink from the oak-covered ledge next to her, she sipped the fiery bourbon and closed her eyes as the warmth slid down her throat and settled low in her belly. Man, she loved that feeling, it made her feel alive.

Laughter erupted across the bar, boots stamped on the scarred wood floor, and the oak door slammed. A slow smile slid across her face. The place was finally filling up, which meant she'd be shooting some pool soon. She eyed the small group that had walked in—four men and a woman. They pulled up to a tall table on the other side of the half wall where she stood. She didn't recognize these folks, which wasn't unusual this time of year; the Derby brought in loads of new faces. The group was clearly friends as they jovially teased and taunted each other while their drinks were served. She kind of envied that. She had a couple of close friends, but these days they didn't get together much. Toni had gotten married about ten years ago and had three adorable—but very busy—children. She was running from dance class to band practice to baseball and back around again. They spoke on the phone often and about once a quarter they managed a night out when Toni's husband, Al, managed to wrangle the kids to give her some girl time.

The woman had a small build, long dark hair and dark eyes, and was exotic in a wholesome sort of way. Tomboyish. She wore jeans, a long deep blue T-shirt that hugged her slight curves and she wore what looked like Army boots. She had a colorful full-sleeve tattoo on her right arm of red roses. It was stunning.

One of the men seemed to be her man as he hung his arm around her shoulders in more than a casual way. His sandy brown hair was laced with silver, and he had a deep scar on his forearm. Then he leaned in and kissed her, and the way they looked into each other's eyes afterward made Stevie's stomach clench just a bit. She sipped the warm amber liquid in her glass and let the fire settle the churning.

A large blond man, easily six foot four or five and broad as a barn, seemed almost shy as he stood with the group, but yet, held himself slightly aloof. His hair curled at the collar and was long around the ears. He was either growing it out or sorely in need of a cut. His blue eyes held intelligence but he seemed a bit unsure of himself.

The smaller man of the group wore short, cropped blond hair and had the most stunning blue eyes she'd ever seen. His easy laugh and jolly disposition made her smile, and she watched with rapt attention as he teased the other man in the group. Now that one—mmm. He was fine. Mighty fine.

Six foot two or so with dark, sultry eyes and hair. Silver strands glinted in the light when he turned his head. He jovially nudged the shorter man with his elbow and laughed. Oh my! His full lips lifted and the dimples popped out. On both sides. Yowza! He glanced her way and the look he laid on her damn near melted her panties. Holy hell! He nodded, then picked up his drink, and she couldn't stop watching his Adam's apple bob as he swallowed the amber liquid—the same color as hers, incidentally—in his glass. He probably drove a big-ass pickup truck and a motorcycle. He'd look killer driving either.

"Another one, Stevie?" the bubbly waitress, oddly named Schmoo, loudly chirped.

She turned to her right and assessed Schmoo. She had bright, curly-red hair and freckles strewn across her nose and cheeks. She wore bib overall shorts and white socks pushed down to the top of her brown, construction-type boots. The younger woman looked twelve; but, of course, she had to be older to serve alcohol, but damned if you could tell.

"Yep. Why is everyone so late getting here today?"

Schmoo looked around as if she'd just noticed the bar was emptier than usual.

"Carnival pulled in a while ago, so you know..." She shrugged her shoulders. "Folks love to go gawk at the carnies. They'll be around soon."

Schmoo strutted away as if she were a dancer, light on her feet—even in boots.

Stevie smiled as she watched the red curls bouncing about her head. That girl could put you in a good mood just looking at her.

"You shooting or just holding up the wall?"

Before she could grasp the situation, her nipples puckered to sharp points, and moisture gathered between her legs. She turned to see the tall, dark drink of water standing in her space, shadowing her from the light. He smelled heavenly, like expensive aftershave and the combination of the aroma and the deep, slow, sultry voice rose the gooseflesh on her arms.

She swallowed to moisten her throat. Then swallowed again, because just being this close to him did funny things to her. "Shootin'. For a buck and a drink. Last pocket," she managed to say, proud of herself for not stammering.

He nodded once and bent to slide his four quarters into the pool table coin slot. Pushing in and releasing, the loud crack of balls hitting the rails and rolling toward the end signaled it was playtime. She watched as his muscles straining under the gray T-shirt bunched and flattened as he gracefully pulled the pool balls from their landing place and laid them into the triangle. He stood and rearranged the balls sorting the solids from the stripes and bunching them together with his hands. She couldn't stop looking at the way his thick, long fingers danced across the balls.

He turned and caught her gaze with his, and the burning in her stomach had nothing to do with the bourbon this time. The man was positively smoldering.

She walked to the other end of the pool table, as much to break as to put some space between her and the dark, mysterious man breathing the same air as she. She leaned down, eyed her mark and cracked the cue with the white ball, sending the colorful balls in all directions, but not dropping anything into a pocket. Shit.

She nodded to him. He smirked then proceeded to bend over the table and sink three balls into various pockets. All solids. The sting of not getting the first ball in was tempered by the sight of his fine ass as he smoothly draped his form over the table. She'd bring this one to his knees later when she stripped for him and proceeded to have her way with his body. Yep, that was her new plan now. Pool didn't hold the same appeal anymore. She'd been celibate for far too long now, and it was time to have a little fun. She sent up a silent prayer, Thank you, Lord, for bringing someone interesting into Bourbonville.

The game continued, mostly in silence, unless one or the other of them needed to call a pocket. Their subtle mating dance, preening and stretching before each other, was the only other thing going on in the room. Her attention was constantly diverted from her game as she watched his panther-like movements stalk the table and sink each ball in one by one. He always watched the exits as he stood and before he bent, a quick glance telling her he was probably military or ex-military. Always vigilant.

His scent floated over her once more as he walked past, leaned down, and sunk the eight ball into the last pocket. He laid his cue on the table and slowly turned to her as he crooned, "I'll take bourbon – Ethan's new blend."

Their eyes met, and the heat climbed her body,

staining her cheeks as a shiver ran amok to the tips of her
toes. Damn. He wore a slight smile on his face as his dark
eyes raked over her face and her breasts before landing on
her lips. The intensity of his stare made her nipples
pucker again, and her breath came in spurts. His expen-
sive-smelling cologne floated over her, and she had a hard
time moving. She wanted to squeeze her thighs closed,
but that would be obvious. Then he spoke, and the deep,
rich tone damn near made her lose it.

"Sam. My friends call me Mac." He held his hand out
to her, and it took her a few moments to come back to
earth.

"Stevie. My friends call me Stevie." Her hand grasped
his and her fingers wrapped around his firmly, pumping
twice before stopping. The heat of his hand ran up her
arm, and she shivered.

"So, Stevie isn't short for anything?" he teased. A slow
smile slid across his handsome face. His deep brown eyes
twinkled in the dim light of the poolroom.

Her heartbeat raced, and the air left her lungs when
she heard his low chuckle.

"Yes." Her voice cracked. She swallowed and tried
again. "Stephanie."

He nodded his head once, never looking away from
her, then released her hand. The loss left her wanting
more. His gaze slid down her body, and it felt like the hot
lick of a tongue. When his eyes made the trip back to hers,
he leaned against the pool table, resting his fine ass on the
edge, and crossed his arms over his chest.

She managed a smile with her trembling lips and
nodded once as she found a way to make her feet move
toward the bar to buy his drink.

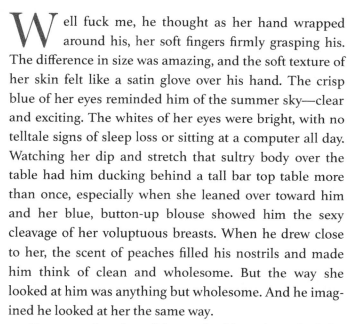

Well fuck me, he thought as her hand wrapped around his, her soft fingers firmly grasping his. The difference in size was amazing, and the soft texture of her skin felt like a satin glove over his hand. The crisp blue of her eyes reminded him of the summer sky—clear and exciting. The whites of her eyes were bright, with no telltale signs of sleep loss or sitting at a computer all day. Watching her dip and stretch that sultry body over the table had him ducking behind a tall bar top table more than once, especially when she leaned over toward him and her blue, button-up blouse showed him the sexy cleavage of her voluptuous breasts. When he drew close to her, the scent of peaches filled his nostrils and made him think of clean and wholesome. But the way she looked at him was anything but wholesome. And he imagined he looked at her the same way.

He sat on the edge of the pool table and watched the fine sway of her ass as she walked to the bar, pulling money from her back pocket as she made her way across the scarred wooden floor. She chatted with the bartender, Ethan Hastings, one of the bar's owners, turned to lock eyes with him, then turned away again. Ethan chuckled, his blue eyes darting around the room as he poured drinks—never missing a beat. Stevie picked up the two glasses of Bourbon and walked toward him, her ample breasts swaying slightly.

Their fingers brushed as he took his drink from her hand, and her pupils grew making her baby blues deepen. Her mouth opened and he thought he detected a sigh. Perfect! He hadn't been laid since he'd rolled into this town three months ago—dry spell over.

He held his glass up, "Salud," then tapped it to hers and sipped.

He watched over the rim as she drank down a healthy mouthful, her eyes slid closed, and a soft smile graced her face. When her eyes opened she looked straight into his; her expression changed from serene to humorous as her smile widened.

"I love feeling the warm slide," she admitted. The quality of her voice reminded him of Kathleen Turner— low and smoldering.

Ah, yes, his cue. He leaned forward and whispered, "I've got another warm slide I think you'll enjoy just as much." This time there was no mistaking the shiver that slithered down her body, his eyes instantly slid to her breasts, and he saw the peaked nipples slightly through her bra. She was going to be fun.

Her voice deepened. "I'll bet you do," she husked. "I think you'll enjoy it just as much as I will."

His nostrils flared, and he breathed in deeply, inhaling the peachy scent and quickly growing impatient. "Let's go."

Her smile widened. She kicked back the remaining spirits and gracefully set her glass on the half wall. Her brows raised as she stared into his. A slow smile spread across her face, mocking him, maybe daring him. He didn't need more than that. He slammed back his drink, set his empty glass next to hers, then glanced back at his friends and waved. Stevie took his hand in hers and led him through the poolroom and down the short hallway to the back door. Stepping from the dark bar into the late afternoon sunlight caused him to blink. He briefly glanced around and saw no vehicles in sight, the back lot nothing more than enough space for three cars, at most, and the dumpster area. The dark wood siding would need a coat of paint in the next year or so, but the air smelled oddly fresh—like laundry detergent.

He eagerly followed without speaking, his need growing as he hungrily watched her ass moving with each step, hampering the long strides he wanted to take to anywhere, so he could slide into her. She glanced back once, her blonde hair swishing over her shoulders, a sexy smile opening her lips. Her hand squeezed his and tugged him forward as if she were more eager than he. Highly unlikely.

They crossed the alley, their footsteps crunching on the gravel. The late afternoon sun still brightened the sky, and the halo that formed around her head caused him to chuckle.

She looked back, "What are you laughing at?"

He shook his head. "The sun cast a halo around your head."

She laughed, and it was akin to a perfect melody. His stomach twisted. "Honey, I'm no angel," she silkily replied, and he stumbled.

She giggled and tugged harder. Reaching into her front pocket, she pulled out a key attached to a little horseshoe. She held it up for him to see then pointed to an upstairs apartment, a little wooden deck protruding from the red brick building. She unlocked a door and stepped inside. "Turn the lock behind you please." She let go of his hand as she climbed the stairs. Nice view.

He turned, twisted the lock and followed just far enough behind that her derriere was directly in front of his face. The old wooden steps creaked and groaned as his weight moved from one to the next, the little enclosed staircase lit only by the windows situated every fourth step or so. No decorations brightened the area; nothing made it feel like a home.

She unlocked the door at the top of the steps and stepped into the apartment. He was pleasantly surprised as he entered behind her. The light tan walls were decorated with pictures of beautiful purebred horses; one of them running along a fence line, three professionally framed photos of horses standing at the grandstand, a ring of roses slung around their necks, their nostrils flared as the pride in their eyes gleamed back at him. She set her key on the oak table, and he couldn't help but notice the crystals embedded into the horseshoe. Her apartment smelled like fresh laundry soap and fabric softener.

"You need something to drink?" she silkily asked.

He turned to her and watched as she slowly unbuttoned her blouse. He was mesmerized by her nimble fingers, and she made short work of each one. "No," was all he could manage.

He pulled his gray T-shirt from his jeans and swiftly pulled it over his head. Draping it over the back of one of the upholstered kitchen chairs, he leaned down and untied his work boots, watching as she did the same. She finished first and pushed her boots toward the wall under the picture of a sprawling ranch surrounded by horses.

Standing, she unhooked her bra, a slow sexy smile gracing her face. She let it fall to her hands, then slowly turned and walked to a door and disappeared into another room. Damn.

He fumbled with his boot laces, finished pulling them from his feet, shoved his socks into his boots and followed the sexy siren calling him from the other room. His motor was revved to a hundred miles per hour.

This concludes your sneak peek at Finish Line, Bluegrass Security Book Two. To continue reading about Mac and Stevie, grab your copy here: https://www.pjfiala.com/books/finish-line-bluegrass-security/

ALSO BY PJ FIALA

Click here to see a list of all of my books with the blurbs.

Contemporary Romance

Rolling Thunder Series

Moving to Love, Book 1

Moving to Hope, Book 2

Moving to Forever, Book 3

Moving to Desire, Book 4

Moving to You, Book 5

Moving Home, Book 6

Second Chances Series

Designing Samantha's Love, Book 1

Securing Kiera's Love, Book 2

Military Romantic Suspense

Bluegrass Security Series

Heart Thief, Book One

Finish Line, Book Two

Lethal Love, Book Three

Big 3 Security

Ford: Finding His Fire Book One

Lincoln: Finding His Mark Book Two

Dodge: Finding His Jewel Book Three

Rory: Finding His Match Book Four

GHOST

Defending Keirnan, GHOST Prequel

Defending Sophie, GHOST Book One

Defending Roxanne, GHOST Book Two

Defending Yvette, GHOST Book Three

GET A FREE EBOOK!

Building a relationship with my readers is the very best thing about writing. I send monthly newsletters with details on new releases, special offers and other fun things relating to my books or prizes surrounding them.

If you sign up to my mailing list I'll send you:

1. A copy of Moving to Love, Book 1 of the Rolling Thunder series.

2. A book list so you know what order to read my books in.

You can get Moving to Love **for free**, by signing up at https://www.subscribepage.com/PJsReadersClub_copy

MEET PJ

Writing has been a desire my whole life. Once I found the courage to write, life changed for me in the most profound way. Bringing stories to readers that I'd enjoy reading and creating characters that are flawed, but lovable is such a joy.

When not writing, I'm with my family doing something fun. My husband, Gene, and I are bikers and enjoy riding to new locations, meeting new people and generally enjoying this fabulous country we live in.

I come from a family of veterans. My grandfather, father, brother, two sons, and one daughter-in-law are all veterans. Needless to say, I am proud to be an American and proud of the service my amazing family has given.

PJ is the author of the exciting Rolling Thunder series, Bounty Hunters, Second Chances and Chandler County series. Soon, her GHOST series will be exciting readers with page turning military alphas and the women who love them.

Her online home is https://www.pjfiala.com. You can connect with PM on Facebook at https://www.facebook.com/PJFialaI, on Twitter at @pfiala and Instagram at https://www.Instagram.com/PJFiala. If you prefer to email, go ahead, she'll respond - pjfiala@pjfiala.com.

SAPPHIRE FALLS

Now that you've fallen in love with Sapphire Falls, you can go back again and again!
There are so many more stories, along with more about the people, places, and traditions at www. SapphireFalls.net
Titles in the Sapphire Falls series by Erin Nicholas:
Main Series:
Getting out of Hand
Getting Worked Up
Getting Dirty
Getting It All
Getting Lucky
Getting Over It
Getting His Way

Holiday collection:
Getting In the Spirit
Getting In the Mood
Getting to the Church on Time (wedding novella)

After Hours series:
After All
After You
After Tonight

Made in the USA
Coppell, TX
06 August 2022

80988535R00121